Kissing
FATHER
CHRISTMAS

ALSO BY ROBIN JONES GUNN

Finding Father Christmas
Engaging Father Christmas

Available from FaithWords wherever books are sold.

Kissing
FATHER
CHRISTMAS

A NOVEL

ROBIN JONES GUNN

New York   Boston   Nashville

Copyright © 2016 by Robin's Nest Productions, Inc.
Reading group guide copyright © 2016 by Robin's Nest Productions, Inc. and Hachette Book Group, Inc.
Cover design by JuLee Brand. Cover illustration by Mark Stutzman. Cover copyright © 2016 by Hachette Book Group, Inc.

FaithWords
Hachette Book Group
1290 Avenue of the Americas
New York, NY 10104
www.faithwords.com
twitter.com/faithwords

First Edition: October 2016

FaithWords is a division of Hachette Book Group, Inc. The FaithWords name and logo are trademarks of Hachette Book Group, Inc.

The publisher is not responsible for websites (or their content) that are not owned by the publisher.
The Hachette Speakers Bureau provides a wide range of authors for speaking events. To find out more, go to www.hachettespeakersbureau.com or call (866) 376-6591.

Library of Congress Cataloging-in-Publication Data
Names: Gunn, Robin Jones, 1955- author.
Title: Kissing Father Christmas : a novel / Robin Jones Gunn.
Description: First edition. | New York : FaithWords, 2016.
Identifiers: LCCN 2016022186| ISBN 9781455565603 (hardcover) | ISBN
    9781478913382 (audio book) | ISBN 9781455565580 (ebook)
Subjects: LCSH: Man-woman relationships--Fiction. | Dating (Social
    customs)--Fiction. | BISAC: FICTION / Christian / Romance. | GSAFD:
    Christian fiction. | Love stories.
Classification: LCC PS3557.U4866 K57 2016 | DDC 813/.54--dc23 LC record available at
·https://lccn.loc.gov/2016022186

ISBNs: 978-1-4555-6560-3 (hardcover), 978-1-4555-6558-0 (ebook)

Printed in the United States of America

RRD-C

10 9 8 7 6 5 4 3 2 1

For Marlene, Sandy, Stephanie, and Bill

Your unwavering faith in the true
Father of Christmas ignites your
vision for what could be.
The four of you inspired this story
without even knowing it.

Kissing
FATHER
CHRISTMAS

Chapter One

J awoke as the pale light of the December morn was finding its way into the upstairs guest room at Whitcombe Manor. The heavy drapes appeared to be etched with a silver lining that trailed like a single thread across the dark wood floor. I propped myself up in the cozy bed and folded my lily-white blond hair into a loose braid, letting it cascade over my shoulder. A contented smile rested on my lips in the hushed room.

I'm really here. I'm back in England.

This place, these people, had been in my waking dreams ever since I came to the enchanting village of Carlton Heath for my cousin's wedding last May. Ian was raised in Scotland, so I'd never met him. His mother passed away several years ago and his fiancée, Miranda, did something I'd never seen before. She included a personal note with their formal wedding invitation. The last line really got to me.

*It would mean the world to Ian and me if you could be with us
on our special day and represent Ian's mother's side of the family.*

Somehow I convinced my mother to make the trek and honor
the memory of her sister. We stayed at Whitcombe Manor, the
gorgeous estate that had belonged to Miranda's family for gener-
ations. It turned into a life-altering experience for both of us. For
me, Ian and Miranda's wedding day was the stuff of fairy tales. And
I have long been a dreamer and a secret believer in fairy tales.

The men wore dress kilts. Miranda's shimmering white gown
had the longest train I'd ever seen. The storybook couple whispered their vows inside a quaint sandstone chapel while holding
hands in front of a glowing stained glass window. Bagpipes
played as they exited beneath a bower of woven forest greens
dotted with dozens of fragrant, deep red roses. Their reception
was held in the gardens at Whitcombe Manor. All the guests kept
smiling at them as they danced until the first stars came out to
watch them, to bless them.

I fell in love with love that day.

In my twenty-six years as a sheltered only child, I'd never
dreamed of so much beauty and such elegantly expressed affection. My parents were practical and efficient and held to the
notion that feelings should be kept to oneself and all artistic expressions were for private reflection only. They were minimalists
when it came to celebrating birthdays and holidays.

That's why I had never danced before. At least not in public.
But at Ian and Miranda's wedding as the stars looked on, everything changed. I knew then that one day I would return to

Carlton Heath. I would once again stay at Whitcombe Manor. Love would draw me back.

Today was that day.

The morning light now infiltrated all the open crevices around the drapes in my guest room. I tossed back the puffy down comforter and padded over to the grand picture window. With a hearty tug I pulled back the thick fabric and watched the room fill with soft light. A puff of swirling dust particles spun in midair.

The garden below that had hosted Ian and Miranda's glorious wedding reception on that pristine day last May now slumbered in a state of deep resignation. The hollyhocks, foxgloves, and vivid pink cosmos were gone. The lights and lanterns as well as the party tables that had been covered in crisp, white linen had been taken down. All that remained were rows of shorn rosebushes and mounds of waiting perennials.

I stared through the thick-paned window, narrowing my eyes and trying to remember the colors, the music, and the expression of sincere intrigue in Peter's pale blue eyes when he held out his hand to me. Every detail of that dreamy night returned to my mind's eye, starting with the moment when Uncle Andrew drew me out on the dance floor in the middle of the festivities. He spun me around with a great bellowing of Scottish pride for his son and new daughter-in-law and I laughed at the sheer boldness of his demeanor.

I felt welcomed into the clan and gladly entered in when Miranda motioned for me to join a circle of young women. We were all soon laughing and holding hands as we jigged forward into a close huddle and then hopped back to expand the circle and invite others to join in. We were like the Midsummer's Eve fairies I'd read about as a child. In my elation, I motioned for my mother to come join us, but she would not.

She watched me from a corner table as if I were someone she'd never met before.

The jig concluded and I chose to take my slice of cake and enjoy it at Uncle Andrew's table. I sat beside his new wife, Katharine, whom I liked very much. She and I sipped tea from china cups and I decided in that moment that these were my people. I had been born into the wrong branch of our family tree. I had grown up in the wrong country.

In the wake of that epiphany, I looked up and saw tall, gregarious Peter Elliott striding across the garden in his best man's kilt and dress jacket. He was coming to me, coming for me.

He held out his hand in a wordless invitation, and without hesitation I placed mine in his. In the glow of a dozen swaying lanterns, we danced. We danced and danced and I was forever changed. His short brown hair and athletic build were instantly fixed in my memory.

As we danced I thought I saw a touch of sadness in the corner of his eyes, and that hint of vulnerability endeared him to me. I hadn't seen it the night before at the rehearsal dinner. At the restaurant he had been the rowdy life of the party with great stories to tell about Ian since the two of them had been friends so long. The camaraderie between Peter and my cousin was impressive. Ian and Miranda trusted Peter and I did, too, when I let him lead me to the dance floor.

Even now I closed my eyes and swayed in front of the guest

room window as I remembered how warm his hand felt as he rested it on the small of my back and our eyes did their own sort of dance, connecting for a shy, momentary gaze and then pulling away. We slow danced with our lips drawn up in thin, half-moon slivers.

One dance, then two, then a third and a fourth. We conversed in sparse paragraphs, asking each other about jobs and family and both saying what a beautiful night it was.

The last dance began and Peter asked how long I was staying in Carlton Heath. I said we were leaving in two days.

"Two days? That's not much of a visit," he murmured. "You really should stay on."

"I'd love to stay longer but I can't."

He held me a little tighter. We danced until the music came to a lingering finish, and then it happened.

Peter kissed me.

Chapter Two

A quick tap sounded on the guest room door, jolting me out of my daydream by the picture window. I jumped back into bed and snuggled under the comforter.

"Anna? Are you awake?" Ellie, my spritely, red-haired hostess, entered carrying a breakfast tray that appeared entirely too large for her petite frame. Ellie would manage it with aplomb, of course, just as she managed everything else at Whitcombe Manor. She was Miranda's sister-in-law and like Miranda, Ellie had found her place within the clan of the late Sir James Whitcombe. His fame as an actor was known internationally but his extended family had carved out an admirably normal and fairly private sort of life in this quiet village.

"I'm not too early, am I? I thought you might like a cup of tea." With a twist of her foot, Ellie closed the door behind her and placed the breakfast tray on the bedside table. "How was your sleep? Good, I hope. Shall I pour?"

Before I could answer, Ellie was filling the china teacup on the tray with steaming, dark breakfast tea. Two slices of dry toast awaited in a stand-up holder along with a small dish of jam.

"You really didn't have to bring breakfast up here for me."

"Of course I did. It's your first morning. We must welcome you with at least some manners. I dare say, though, that before the week is out you will undoubtedly find yourself foraging around in the kitchen like the rest of us when hunger strikes."

I smiled and took the china cup and held the saucer in my open palm.

Ellie lowered herself into the comfy-looking chair in the corner. "I do hope someone has told you how the week before Christmas turns into complete chaos around here when it comes to mealtimes. I'm sure you've heard about the play at the community theater and the lovely receptions that come with it. Christmas day is always the main event and we're so glad you're here with us this year."

"I'm glad to be here, too. Thanks again for letting me stay with you. I hope I won't be a bother with everything else you have going on."

"*Don't be silly*, Anna. You're family."

I wasn't sure that being the cousin of her sister-in-law's husband qualified me as "family" in the prestigious Whitcombe lineage, but the truth was, those were the exact words I hoped I'd hear when I returned to Carlton Heath.

"I will say that it took no small effort on my part to convince Miranda and Katharine and Andrew to let me keep you here instead of with either of them." Ellie adjusted the wide green scarf that held back her wavy hair. "You've been to Rose Cottage so you know how tight the quarters are at Ian and Miranda's place. And as for Andrew and Katharine's nest above the Tea Cosy...well, it only made sense for you to stay with us since this will be the hub of so many of the Christmas comings and goings."

"Well, I appreciate it." I took a sip of the soothing tea. "And I hope you'll let me help out wherever I can. I meant it when I said it last night. Put me to work while I'm here."

Ellie's face took on an impish expression. "In that case, I do have a favor to ask of you."

"Of course. Anything."

"I should first tell you that this request is my secret Christmas wish and only you can make it come true." She put her hand over her heart as if to emphasize the sincerity of her plea.

"Oh my!" I gave her a teasing grin. "A secret Christmas wish. Sounds intriguing."

"It's about your drawings. Edward and I were impressed with the handmade thank-you note you left for us after the wedding. Your watercolor image of our garden was lovely. So lovely. I showed it to Miranda and she told me about the illustrations you did on those children's books. I was able to hunt down four of them and Julia absolutely adores them. So do I."

I felt my face warming. I wasn't used to receiving compliments on my artwork. At home in Minnesota I kept quiet about my invisible career. All six of the books I'd worked on didn't even list my name as the illustrator because they were all work-for-hire projects. People who'd known me all my life thought I simply lived with my parents so that I could help care for my invalid grandfather. I did help out with Opa, but I also had a small, budding career as a freelance illustrator.

"Edward and I discussed it," Ellie said, switching to a confident-sounding business voice. "We would like to commission you to do a series of sketches of Whitcombe Manor. It's been over a hundred years since any drawings have been made. Our plan is to use them for our letterhead and perhaps for other commercial purposes."

"I'm honored that you asked, Ellie. I'd be happy to make as many drawings as you'd like."

Ellie clapped her hands and grinned wildly. "Wonderful! Edward thinks we shouldn't bother you about working on them during this visit since it is Christmas, after all. Would you be willing to return and stay with us again? We'd cover all your expenses and you could stay as long as you wish."

I felt tiny glistening tears forming in my eyes over the joy I felt at Ellie's invitation.

"I'd love to come back. But I can start working on the sketches this week if you'd like."

"Would you? Yes, I'd like that very much. Is there anything you need?"

"I don't think so. I brought my pencils and sketch pads with me."

"I'm so pleased. Edward will be delighted." Ellie popped up from the chair. "I'm going to tell him right now and leave you to your tea and toast. Take your time. We'll be in the kitchen. Julia and I are making cranberry orange bread this morning for the cast supper this evening."

Ellie blew me a kiss and swished out the door. The green scarf tied around her short, amber hair trailed behind her like the tail of an elf's cap.

I reached for a slice of toast and smiled. Sketches of Whitcombe Manor may have been Ellie's secret Christmas wish, but being invited to return again, before I'd even been in England for twenty-four hours, was mine.

Well, one of my secret Christmas wishes. The other wish involved a certain best man who had been, shall we say, conservative in his communication with me over the past seven months. Peter's most recent e-mail simply said,

> I'm glad you're coming.
> I look forward to seeing you.

I made the mistake of sharing his e-mail with my mother. She thought his words were too noncommittal and suggested I consider canceling my trip so that I didn't run the risk of making a fool of myself.

"You're turning into a feathery sort of woman, Anna. Don't you see how dangerous it is to put yourself in such a vulnerable position?"

What my mother hadn't realized was that I wanted to be a "feathery" woman. Ever since the wedding, I had been inching my way out of the cocoon she and my father had so carefully constructed around my life. I was more than ready to flutter away and was way past the normal stage when it's a healthy choice to release the deeply embedded need for my parents' approval. My flights of fancy resembled the route of a homing pigeon more than the expansive and graceful loops of an artistic butterfly.

But in my heart, I knew I was a butterfly. I was an artist and my "family" in England recognized that, even if my own parents still found my chosen vocation to be unstable and disappointing. I was free and capable and ready to become the woman God hand-crafted me to be.

What my mother also failed to understand was that Peter had been the catalyst for my metamorphosis. I had every reason to believe he would be as eager to pick up where we left off as I was.

I look forward to seeing you. That's what he said in his e-mail. *My being here means as much to him as it does to me.*

I took a nimble bite of my jam-slathered toast and gathered all my hopeful thoughts around me like a fan club. *You'll see, Mother. All your fears are unfounded.*

Chapter Three

$\mathcal{I}$ wasted no time starting on the sketches of Whitcombe Manor.

As soon as I'd helped Ellie and her daughter, Julia, pop the pans of Christmas bread into the oven, I bundled up, collected my sketch pad and pencils, and settled into the comfortable garden chair Edward had set up for me in the front yard.

The sunlight filtered through the trees behind me, giving the face of Whitcombe Manor an enchanting glow.

Seven-year-old Julia joined me as my self-appointed assistant. Just like her mother, Julia was all sweetness, clever ideas, and boundless energy. She spread a blanket at my feet and contentedly combed the tail of her toy pony while telling me about her older brother, Markie, and how he never came along when she and her mum went into London for Christmas shopping.

"We are going to London this week. Did you know that? Miranda is coming with us. Will you come with us, too, Anna? Mummy and I always go to tea at Harrods. It's our favorite tradition."

"It sounds like a very nice tradition."

"Well, we actually only had tea there one time before, on my birthday, but now it's our tradition. We're going to go Christmas shopping and then have tea."

"How fun."

"Oh, it's very fun. You have to come with us. Please!"

"Yes. Of course. I'd love to come."

"Goodie!" Julia looked up at me as I tried to get the outline of the turret just right. "My daddy says you're quite talented, you know."

"No, I didn't know that."

"He said he was glad you were coming for Christmas because this house must always have an artist and that's why you're here."

"Is that right?"

"I like all the books you made very, very much, but you know that because I already told you that when we were baking." She paused before changing topics slightly. "Did you know that my great-great-great-great-great-grandfather who built this house was an artist and his friends came here to paint?"

I was pretty sure Julia had gone a few too many *greats* past the mid-Victorian era when Whitcombe Manor was built, but I did know about Rossetti and the Pre-Raphaelite Brotherhood, which was the group of artists to which she referred.

"I've seen some of their paintings," Julia said. "In a museum in London. Have you been to see their paintings in any museums in London?"

13

"No. Not yet." I took my eyes off the sketch and smiled at Julia. Her wispy brown hair fluttered around her pixie face.

"Am I bothering you? Mummy said I'm not to bother you."

"No, you're not bothering me. Not at all."

"Good." Julia popped up and came over and stood by my side. Instead of examining the sketch, she seemed to examine me. "Do you ever wear your hair flowing down like a princess?"

I chuckled. "Like a princess, huh?"

"Yes, because you already look like a princess because you're so pretty. But you also have very long hair."

"Yes, I do have long hair, don't I?"

"I wondered," Julia said, taking on a coquettish stance in front of me. "Do you ever let anyone brush your hair or make braids in it?"

"Would you like to braid my hair?"

Julia's eyes grew wide. "Could I? Really?"

"Yes. Unless it distracts me from my work." I put on a stern look that didn't seem to fool her one bit.

"I won't keep you from your work. I promise. I'm very good at braids."

I undid my hair and let it hang down over the back of the chair.

"I want my hair to grow as long as yours." Julia gently smoothed her small hand down my mane. "I would brush it every morning and every night."

A sweet memory floated over me as I remembered all the bedtimes when I sat cross-legged on the end of my bed and my mother would brush my hair.

Julia looked over my shoulder at the sketch pad. "Anna, what if you were in the turret of our house and you couldn't get out? You could let down your hair like Rapunzel and the handsome prince would climb up and rescue you."

I smiled and kept sketching. At that moment my childhood bedroom in Minnesota seemed far away. I found it easy to believe in castles and princes and dreams about to come true. It made me happy that Julia shared my love of all things fanciful and enchanting.

As Julia did her styling, I could tell that instead of folding my hair into a single braid, she was adorning me with a haphazard assortment of small braids going every which direction. When she ran out of the ties she used on her pony, she pulled a long pink strand of yarn from the frayed edge of her sweater. She then made use of the rubber bands that held my pencils together.

She tugged a little too much as she secured a tight, thin braid that felt as if it were sprouting out the side of my head above my left ear. I was finding it impossible to draw but I didn't have the heart to say anything.

Fortunately, Julia realized she needed more ties and took off in her usual skip-hop-trot manner. I concentrated on getting the lines of the windows on the second floor to come out in accurate proportion to the roof.

From the end of the long gravel driveway came the sound of the front gate opening. I heard the rumble of a sports car engine. A shiny Austin-Healey came into view and stopped directly in front of the house. The top was down despite the chilly weather and a bicycle protruded from the passenger side.

Everything around me seemed to hush. The driver opened the door, got out, and tossed his cap onto the front seat. My heart fluttered like a butterfly going around in dizzying circles.

Peter!

He turned and gazed across the lawn. I knew he saw me. For a moment, I held my breath. I didn't move. I'd practiced what I'd say when I saw him but at the moment all those clever, rehearsed lines escaped me.

All I could think was, *My hair!*

Chapter Four

$\mathscr{I}$ quickly fumbled to undo Julia's handiwork as Peter strode across the lawn. He was smiling. I smiled back and felt a flush of embarrassment racing up my neck. I could only imagine how I must look with a half dozen braids shooting out of my head and my face the shade of a persimmon.

"Hello!" I blurted out while Peter was more than twenty feet away. I would have stood to greet him but I was still balancing the sketchbook on my lap and had wadded up the hair ties into a little ball and was clutching them in the center of my palm. The left side of my head remained a tumble of mini braids.

Peter tilted his head as he approached, as if sizing up the situation. He looked just as I'd remembered. Clean-shaven and fit. His short brown hair was slightly matted from the cap he'd been wearing.

He paused in front of me for a moment and then leaned over to press a whisper of a kiss just above my right ear. It was awkward but sweet. I didn't grow up in a community that greeted each other with friendly kisses, so when my mother and I were welcomed that way at the wedding by nearly every one of Ian and Miranda's relatives and friends, it took us both by surprise.

"Hello," I repeated.

In the back of my mind, all I could hear was a string of admonitions my mother had repeated to me throughout my childhood. *Don't be forward. Be careful around men. You, more than most women, will have to learn to discern the intentions of any man who stares at you.*

Her cautions made sense when I was young. It was because all the best traits of her Swedish heritage began to blossom in me at an early age. My blue eyes, white-blond hair, and uncomplicated Scandinavian complexion would always cause me to stand out in a crowd. She had delicately warned me that men would stare at me.

Peter was definitely staring at me now. But I had a feeling it was for other reasons. He seemed nervous, too, which surprised me.

"How was your flight?" he asked.

"Good."

"That's good."

He glanced down at the sketch pad. "May I have a look?"

I carefully handed it to him. "Ellie asked if I'd do some drawings for her. It's only a start."

I fiddled with the remaining octopus braids, trying to undo the last ones while he continued to examine the rough sketch.

"Nice. Very nice." Peter handed the pad back with an approving nod and looked at my hair.

"Julia," I said, holding out the tight braid above my ear. I hoped the simple explanation was all that was needed. I knew that Peter had a sister who was much younger than him. I'd met Molly the day after the wedding when he was taking her on a bike ride. Certainly he knew something about the fanciful doings of little girls.

"She went inside to get more ties," I added.

"Then by all means, don't undo her handiwork on my account." Peter grinned that half grin of his and I felt myself beginning to relax.

"I suppose you have a lot of plans while you're here," he said.

"No, not really. I mean, not yet."

"I'm sure that will change once Ian comes back from London this afternoon." Peter glanced back at the car. "I promised I'd leave his car at the station for him. I was on my way but wanted to come by here first."

I smiled, trying to anticipate what he'd say next. It looked like he planned to ride his bike back from the train station, so it wasn't likely that he was about to invite me to go along for the ride. Perhaps he was going to ask me to do something afterward or later that evening.

"Listen, Anna." He looked uneasy and I tried to understand why it was so unnerving for a guy to ask a woman to go out with him. Certainly Peter knew that I'd say yes.

"I wanted to set the record straight on something that happened at the wedding."

I managed to untangle the final braid and brushed back my hair, giving Peter my full attention.

"After we danced, if you recall, we shared a kiss."

I nodded, finding it cute and sort of funny that he'd said "if you recall."

Does he think I've forgotten it? How could I?

That brief brush of a kiss, as awkward and unexpected as it was, had been reviewed in my memory a hundred times. No, a thousand times. I didn't want Peter to know it, but that kiss was my first kiss.

He looked down at his hands and then back up at me. "I should have said something sooner, but I never found the right moment and I didn't want to write it in an e-mail. But you see, I hoped I didn't give you the wrong message."

"The wrong message?" I repeated.

My expression must have reflected the flash of fear that coursed through me, because he moved closer and in a low and soothing voice said, "It was lovely, mind you. I'm not going to pretend I didn't enjoy it. But..."

I waited.

"I intended to only give you a kiss on the cheek, you understand."

I nodded even though I most definitely did not understand. I thought our lips met because they both wanted to.

"You know how it is here. We say hello and good-bye with a small sort of kiss. So, at the end of our dance I thought you and I were saying good-bye. The error was all mine. I seem to have missed the mark, so to speak."

My heart was pounding wildly and I could feel my face turning red.

Peter looked over his shoulder and both of us spotted Julia hop-skipping her way across the lawn, heading toward us.

"I just wanted to set things right," Peter said quickly. "Since I'm sure we'll be seeing each other quite a lot while you're here. I didn't want us to start off on the wrong impression."

Peter released a nervous laugh. "Or, I guess, I meant to say, start us off on the wrong foot."

I couldn't move. It felt as if seven months of stardust was invisibly showering all around me and I was caught in the downpour without an umbrella to protect my poor little heart.

How could I have been so naive?

Peter glanced back at Julia who was almost upon us and with a tilt of his head he added in a low voice, "You didn't take my actions to mean anything else, did you?"

"No. No, of course not." I looked down at the sketch. It turned into a blurry tangle of unfinished lines as I blinked quickly.

Julia eagerly started chatting away. "Hallo, Peter. Did you bring Molly with you?"

"Not this time. She's at home."

"Is she going with you to the Tea Cosy tonight?"

"No, she won't be there."

"Would you tell her that I'm happy that your family is going to have Christmas with us? And tell her to bring her pony."

"Yes. I'll tell her."

I drew in a stabilizing breath and glanced up. Peter was checking his watch. "I should be going." He caught my eye for a moment and said, "I'll see you tonight, then."

"At the Tea Cosy?"

"Yes. At the Tea Cosy." His parting smile seemed promising.

I nodded and forced what I'm sure was an unconvincing smile.

It was all so confusing. As soon as Peter drove out of sight, I planned to close my sketchbook, collect my pencils, and escape to the guest room where I could set free the tears of embarrassment I was trying so hard to hold back.

"Molly is his sister," Julia informed me. "She has some different kinds of problems but she's my friend. Peter made her a special seat so he can take her on bike rides with him." Julia turned her full attention back to me and squealed. "Oh, no! What happened to your hair?"

I handed her the wad of hair ties I'd been clutching in my fist and said in a strained voice, "Sorry, Julia. I need to go inside for a bit."

"That's okay." Julia sounded very mature all of a sudden. She picked up her pony and took over my vacated throne. "When you're a princess, sometimes you have to go do important things. That's what Miranda told me."

"Miranda is a wise princess." I barely made it across the lawn before my throat closed and the onslaught of all my bruised feelings threatened to overwhelm me. I paused in the alcove trying to compose myself before going inside the home that only a short time earlier had seemed like a castle.

Looking up and blinking back the tears, I saw five words etched over the front door, the motto of Whitcombe Manor.

GRACE AND PEACE RESIDE HERE.

I pressed the latch on the ornately carved front door and entered, dearly hoping those words were true for innocent, "feathery women" like me.

Chapter Five

$\mathcal{I}$ stepped into the stunning entry hall of Whitcombe Manor and felt as I had on my first visit to this extraordinary home. I was welcome here.

The ceiling rose to the top of the grand staircase and beyond. Light poured through the large window above the stair landing, enlivening the dark wood floor and giving the sensation of entering a small cathedral. I saw Ellie coming down the stairs with a large box in her arms. It appeared that she had just finished looping the last garland of Christmas greenery on the stairs. The string of twinkle lights woven through the garlands was lit, adding a festive cheerfulness to the entry.

"Oh, good. I was just about to come find you and see if I could persuade you to help me with one more wee project, as your Uncle Andrew would call it."

"A wee project?" I cleared my throat and pulled my emotions back in check.

"It's for the play. You know how every Christmas we perform *A Christmas Carol* by Dickens?"

"Yes. Miranda told me about it. She said your father-in-law, Sir James, started the tradition."

Ellie was in front of me. "Yes, well, I volunteered to take care of the programs this year and I've fallen behind. Terribly behind. I was hoping you could help me out."

"Of course. What do you need?"

Ellie looked at me more closely. "Are you all right? Your eyes look a bit red. Is it jet lag, do you think? Here I am loading you up with projects and you probably want to be taking a catnap right about now."

"No, I'm all right. I can sleep later." *And cry later.* "What did you want me to help you with?"

"It's the programs, you see." Ellie scrutinized my expression one more time. "Are you certain you don't need to lie down for a bit? We'll be up late at the Tea Cosy, you know."

"What exactly is going on tonight at the Tea Cosy?"

"I thought I mentioned it while we were baking. It's the soup dinner for the cast of the play."

"Oh." I couldn't remember if she'd told me or not. "Are there a lot of people going tonight?"

"I suppose. You can never be sure who will show up. We're going because, as you know, your Aunt Katharine is fighting a bad cold. I told her we'd take care of everything. Miranda is there now, making the soup. Ian is coming later and he said he'd ask Peter to help out. I thought you and I could go around four. Is that all right?"

"Yes. Of course."

Ellie motioned with her head for me to follow her into the study. I was grateful for the distraction as well as the detour from what would have turned into a desperately sad hideaway time in the guest room.

The moment I entered the study I was reminded that there was a long list of reasons besides Peter that had endeared me to this place and to this extended family. The high shelves were stacked full of wonderfully musty-smelling books. The leather chairs, imposing desk, and intricate rugs in this room spoke to me of stories not yet told. Tales of mystery and adventure. I belonged here. This romantic setting was enough to help me rewrite the script in my mind. It would be a different Christmas than I'd hoped for, but it would still be wonderful in many other ways.

Although, Peter will be at the Tea Cosy later.

I set that thought aside and told myself that if I kept all my fanciful thoughts centered on the charm of this old house, the enchantment of the library, and the delight of spending time with Ellie, Miranda, and Julia, my heart would sail through the rest of the visit without any additional bruises.

With my chin raised and shoulders back, I paused in front of one of the photos of Sir James that hung on the wall. He really had been the last of a breed of distinguished, honored British actors. Sir James had convinced the world that handsome gentlemen who drove speedboats, spoke five languages, and wore a tux under a scuba suit were capable of protecting England and her beloved queen from all harm. The allure of his legendary persona lingered in this dusty room.

Ellie put the box down beside one of the wingback chairs and opened the laptop on the large, dark mahogany desk.

"Don't be shocked, but this is all I've got so far." Ellie motioned for me to sit in the chair at the desk and have a look at her open laptop.

It did strike me that it was an extraordinary thing to be casually sitting at Sir James's desk. How many people ever got to do that?

On the screen was the image of a plump couple in Victorian garb. They looked like they were dancing a jig.

"What am I looking at?" I asked.

"It's the Fezziwig's Ball. I had to scan the illustration three times from the book to get it right. Don't tell Edward. He's quite protective of the books around here. That one is a first edition."

I reached for the old book on the desk that she'd pointed to and smoothed my hand over the brown cover. The title *A Christmas Carol* was in gold lettering with a detailed etched wreath circling it. I opened to the title page and checked the copyright date: 1843. I could only imagine the value of a first edition of Dickens's *A Christmas Carol*. Turning to the next page with more care, I smoothed back the tissue that covered the illustration. I recognized the process that had been used on the Fezziwig's Ball drawing and was impressed.

"This is needle and acid etching," I said. "It's beautiful. This is not easy to do." I had to agree with Edward that none of the pages in this valuable book should be scanned three times.

"Are you able to fit that image onto the template for the cover? I had no success in lining it up properly and I'm desperate. The play is only two days away."

"Sure. I can try. Graphic design is not my specialty but I know a few basics."

"If you click on the other open file, you'll see the rest of the information."

I was relieved to see that the interior of the program was completed and that I wouldn't be responsible for listing the names of the cast and crew.

"My thought with the Fezziwig's image was to play off the pensioners. Although you don't call them pensioners in the States, do you? Seniors. Is that right? Those who are in retirement. Last year the cast was all children. It was delightful. This year it's all pensioners. You'll meet them at the Tea Cosy this evening."

All I could think about as I clicked and resized the image to fit the program template was that I shouldn't be thinking about the fact that Peter would be at the Tea Cosy this evening. I tried to convince myself that our uncomfortable conversation was the last awkward moment I'd experience with him. We were both going to be in the same small circles this week. It would be fine. It had to be fine.

I'd almost convinced myself when a paralyzing thought seized me.

My mother was right. I have made a fool of myself by coming here.

I was sure there were worse realizations that could befall a young woman as she's trying to carve out her own life, but at that moment, I couldn't think of anything worse.

I decided that if things went poorly that night when I was around Peter, I'd make up an excuse to have to leave and spend the rest of my trip at a hotel in London. I didn't want to put a strain on any of these lovely people during their Christmas celebration by being the one person in the bunch that Peter would be trying to avoid.

Christmas in London would be wonderful. I could see Big Ben and Buckingham Palace and even visit some of the art museums Julia talked about. The trip to England wouldn't be a waste.

Just a disappointment.

And that would be the most humiliating part of it. I didn't want to go back to Minnesota and admit to my mother that I'd finally grown up and she was right. Capricious dreamers only set themselves up for heartache while solid, forthright women know that fairy tales don't come true.

Chapter Six

$\mathcal{T}$he Tea Cosy was already humming with activity when Ellie and I arrived.

The bells that hung over the front door chimed merrily as we entered the tavern-style café that was built over two hundred years ago. A fire crackled in the soot-stained fireplace. Flickering votive candles dotted the mantel and the welcoming scent of freshly baked bread wafted from the kitchen behind the drawn curtain.

The cast wasn't supposed to come until five o'clock but they had shown up in costume at teatime and had made themselves at home around the tables. The thick wood beams across the low ceiling drew their conversations in close.

I felt as if I'd stepped into a Dickens novel and should be checking the corner for Tiny Tim's stool.

When my uncle Andrew's wife, Katharine, purchased the building several years ago, she did her best to keep as much of the original design as the building inspectors would allow. Her insistence paid off handsomely. The charming Tea Cosy along with the village of Carlton Heath had received top ratings on a popular tourist website that promoted the must-sees of their area.

Miranda appeared from the kitchen with two large, white teapots. As soon as she saw me, she delivered them to the closest tables and sashayed around the tables to get to me. Her dark hair was pulled up and her face was rosy. She wrapped her arms around me and said, "It's so good to have you here, Anna. I can't wait to have a chance to sit down and talk."

"Chatting comes afterward," Ellie said, heading for the kitchen. "We have a dinner to serve."

Miranda took me by the hand and led me through the gauntlet of friendly guests. They wanted to know if I was the "visiting American" and if more tea was on its way.

I was surprised to see how small the kitchen was. I hadn't gone behind the curtain when I visited last May. It was impressive to see how Katharine had made clever use of all possible open space. Ian was stirring one of two large pots of soup. He put the spoon down and slid over to greet me with a kiss on the cheek. His gesture brought an immediate reminder of Peter's explanation of hello and good-bye kisses and the unspoken rule of turning your head.

I immediately took note of the fact that Peter wasn't there. Perhaps he was planning to come later. Or maybe he'd bowed out so that it wouldn't be awkward with me there.

There was no time to chitchat. Ellie and I had brought in three shopping bags of supplies, including the fourteen mini loaves of cranberry orange bread we'd baked that morning.

"Since they've come for tea, let's serve the cranberry bread," Ellie suggested. "Save the rolls for when we serve the soup. Have you pulled out all the teapots, Miranda?"

I pushed up the sleeves on my sweater and pulled my hair back into a knotted ponytail. Miranda pointed me to the teapots and canister of loose tea leaves.

"I think Ellie and I should switch tasks. I'll cut the bread and serve it to the tables. She's better suited to know how to make a pot of tea."

"There's nothing to it," Ellie said. "As long as you always add one more teaspoon for the pot."

I wasn't sure what she meant but I had no trouble falling into sync with the rest of the kitchen crew. The jovial cast all wanted me to linger and talk with their table when I served the small plates with the sliced bread artistically arranged. They wanted to know where I was from, how long I'd be staying, and how I was related to Miranda.

I heard several times that my accent sounded just like Miranda's and I thought that was funny. I responded by saying, "And here I thought you were the one with the accent." They chuckled and guffawed at my response.

I told Miranda what they said when I returned to the kitchen and started stacking up soup bowls next to the stove.

"It feels like I've stepped into an alternate universe each time I go back out there."

Miranda smiled. "What would a group like this be doing in Minnesota right now, do you suppose?"

"They'd probably be playing bingo in the church hall. Or having a white elephant gift exchange and eating way too many Christmas cookies and homemade fudge."

"And let me guess," Miranda added. "The women wouldn't be wearing silly caps with ringlets and fifty-year-old fuzzy sweaters. Instead they'd put on their favorite sweatshirt appliquéd with a Christmas tree and they'd wear headbands with felt reindeer antlers."

I saw her point. The way older people gathered and celebrated in my corner of the world was just as silly if not sillier than the jovial bunch celebrating here in Carlton Heath.

Miranda grinned. "I do love having another American around here. It makes me want to go back to Rose Cottage so we can watch *Elf* and eat candy corns. I miss candy corns."

"Really? You don't have candy corns here?"

"I've not been able to find any. What I miss even more is Ghirardelli chocolate chips. I used to live in San Francisco, so to me there is no better chocolate in the world. I've tried to make chocolate chip cookies here but they just don't taste the same."

"Well then, when I go home, I'll be sure to put together a care package for you with candy corns and lots of Ghirardelli chocolate and send it to you for the new year."

Miranda's expression narrowed. "What makes you think any of us are going to allow you to return to the US?"

"I think British immigration might have a thing or two to say about it."

"You belong here, Anna. One way or another, we'll get you to stay."

I didn't have time to choke up over Miranda's kind words because Ellie had decided that we would move right into serving the soup and rolls. We set up an assembly line, and my task was to carry the soup out to the tables.

I was concentrating so intently on my waitressing skills that I didn't notice when Peter arrived. I only found out he was there when a round of laughter rose from one of the tables by the fire. Peter was using large hand motions as he told them a story. He had the rapt attention of everyone around him. Another round of laughter erupted as I scurried to the kitchen for another tray of soup bowls.

"Peter must have arrived," Ian noted.

"Yes. He's here."

"He always livens up a party," Miranda said.

"Someone go tell him to get in here and liven up our soup service!" Ellie was red in the face as she stood by the stove with a ladle in her hand.

I returned to the dining area with more bowls of soup and shyly glanced over at Peter. He was greeting another table full of cast members and didn't notice me. I didn't want to be the one to activate Ellie's command and try to herd him into the kitchen. He looked so happy. The guests were all happy. I watched him from across the room and made a terrible discovery.

My heart still felt fluttery when I saw him.

This is going to be more difficult than I thought. I have to guard my heart. I have to keep my feelings to myself.

I served a bowl of soup to a woman wearing an odd cap with lots of ringlets bouncing underneath the ruffled edge. She reminded me of Miss Piggy's character of Bob Cratchit's wife in the Muppet version of *A Christmas Carol*. The woman turned to me and said, "Thank you ever so much, sweet Anna."

"You know my name."

"Of course. We all do. Small village, you know. Peter has been telling us about you."

I glanced across the room. Peter's back was toward me. I felt a clenching sensation in my stomach. Exactly what had Peter been telling everyone? Were they laughing because he was relating stories about me? Was it the braids in my hair?

I hurried back to the safety of the kitchen. *He wouldn't be telling them about the way I misinterpreted his kiss at the wedding reception, would he?*

"I need to step outside for a bit of air," I told Miranda. "Do you mind finishing up the soup service? There are only two more tables waiting."

"Sure." Miranda took the tray from me. "Are you feeling all right?"

"Just a little woozy."

"Jet lag can do that to you. Try drinking some water. Better yet, see if there's any orange juice in the refrigerator."

I settled for a glass of water and slipped out the back door of the kitchen onto a small brick patio area where a clothesline was strung from the side of the building to the fence. The sky had darkened and a crisp chill was in the air. It felt like Minnesota on an autumn night. That sense of familiarity comforted me.

I folded my arms across my middle and tilted my head back, staring into the heavens.

What am I going to do?

"Hey, pardon me," a gruff voice called out from the kitchen doorway. "Did you get clearance to come out here on a break?"

Chapter Seven

I turned to see Peter leaning against the doorframe looking like a teenage hooligan with his hands in his pockets and his shoulders rounded forward.

He grinned at me the way he'd grinned last May across the table at the rehearsal dinner. Friendly, joking, slightly bashful, looking like someone who was having a good time at the party.

I played along with his teasing question. "I snuck out. You won't tell on me, will you?"

"Your secret is safe with me." He pulled his hands out of his pockets and strolled over to where I was standing. Tilting his chin up, he scanned the sky above us as if trying to see what I had been looking at.

"Were you out here checking on the universe? Making sure all the moving parts are still working?"

"I was just getting some air." I glanced at him, but he continued to stare at the sky. We still hadn't made eye contact.

"God does a pretty good job of keeping it all in motion, doesn't He?"

"Yes. He does." I was beginning to feel nervous about where this conversation might go, or not go, and added, "I guess we're the ones who get out of sync."

He didn't reply.

I wished I hadn't said that. Peter could easily take that to mean that I was still stuck on the kiss and how I'd misinterpreted it. He was the one who was attempting to normalize our conversation. The least I could do was stick to neutral comments.

"It's a good thing that He keeps extending grace to us, don't you think?"

"Yes."

"We can make a fresh start of it at any time." I could tell that Peter was looking at me. I kept my eyes toward the night sky, not yet willing to let our eyes meet.

"I hope we can do that," he added. "Make a fresh start of it."

I turned slowly and met his gaze in the glow of the dim, yellowed light pouring from the open kitchen door. The earlier tensions and anxious thoughts dissipated.

Offering Peter a warm smile, I said, "Of course. Fresh starts."

"So, we're friends, then?"

"Yes. Friends."

I knew how to be "friends" with a lot of guys. Most of them were married to friends I'd known since childhood. I could start over and be "chums" with Peter. No one needed to ever know about the hopelessly romantic embers I'd kept warming in my heart for him all these months. Being able to talk easily around him was a better alternative than packing my bags and tiptoeing out of this small village in the morning.

"I heard you're thinking of going into London tomorrow," he said.

I must have given him a startled look, as if he'd just read my thoughts.

"With Ellie and Julia," he clarified. "I heard the plan is for Christmas shopping at Harrods and afternoon tea at the Georgian Restaurant."

"Oh, yes. Christmas shopping with Ellie and Julia. I think Miranda is going, too."

"Do you have plans for afterward?"

"I don't know. I don't think so."

"Would you like to see a bit of Londontown while you're there?" Peter cautiously ventured. "I'm going to be in London tomorrow. If you'd like, I could meet you at Harrods after tea and take you around."

"Could you take me to see Ben?"

"Ben?"

"Yeah, the big, tall guy with the handsome face and outstretched hands."

It was clear that Peter hadn't picked up on my attempt at being clever.

"Big Ben," I said plainly. "I've always wanted to see him." Trying out Ellie's cute line from this morning, I added, "It's my Christmas wish."

A look of sudden understanding spread across Peter's face. "Tall guy, open arms. Right. And I bet you're going to tell me that his face lights up when you go see him at night."

"I hope it does. I've yet to meet him."

"You've come to the right tour guide, then, because as a matter of fact, I know where to find him."

"Good." I kept going with the playful, teasing tone. "In that case, I will go with you tomorrow. But only if you promise to take me to see Ben."

Peter was still smiling. "Why do I get the feeling you're one of those women who just uses a guy like me to get close to some other guy like Ben?"

I gave him a grin but didn't have a comeback. I was still trying to figure out where the sassy lines about Big Ben had come from since that wasn't my usual way of speaking to anyone.

Except, I guess that is the way I banter with the husbands of my childhood girlfriends. I somehow always go into a coy mode around them. That's interesting. Is this the only way I know how to feel comfortable interacting with men my age?

"Hallo! There you two are." Ellie stepped outside with a dish towel in her hand. "Are you feeling all right, Anna?"

"Yes. I'm fine. Thanks."

"Any chance we might employ the services of the two of you for the final round?"

"After you," Peter playfully bent at the waist and extended his outstretched arm toward the door. "Ladies first."

The rest of the evening rolled out with lots of laughter and a comfortable camaraderie with the kitchen crew. I chose to refrain from doing much talking because I was still trying to figure out why I turn coy and a bit sassy when I'm trying to communicate with men. It seemed best to just keep smiling and enjoy the company. It was great fun being around Peter and watching how he "worked the floor," as Ian called it.

"I always told him that instead of becoming an architect, he should have taken up a career as a dining room maître d' on a cruise ship." Ian filled the sink with hot water and added more dish soap than needed. "He's at home with an audience—that's for certain."

Tiny incandescent bubbles began rising from the sink. Ian plunged his large hands into the water, releasing even more of the liquid pearls. Miranda and I exchanged quiet grins. Both of us had noticed how the transcending bubbles were clinging to the ends of Ian's light brown hair like the remains of a dismantled halo.

Miranda motioned for me to join her by the stove where she was standing and eating a bowl of soup.

"Did you get anything to eat, Anna?"

"No. I probably should."

"There's soup and some rolls left, but not many. Here." She handed me a freshly washed and dried soup bowl and nodded toward the pan on the stove. "Please help yourself."

"Would anyone else like some?" I asked.

"I'm good," Ellie said. She was drying bowls faster than Ian could wash them.

"None for me," Ian said. "Peter said he ate before he came and I took bowls up to my dad and Katharine earlier. What's left is all yours, Anna."

I was hungrier than I realized and went looking for a remaining roll after I'd finished the soup. Ellie noticed what I was doing.

With a chuckle she said, "Didn't I tell you this morning? We serve you breakfast in bed merely to put on a good front. After that, you're on your own for your meals."

I stuffed the last bite of the last roll into my mouth and chewed contentedly. A little thrill rose inside me, elevating like the iridescent floating soap bubbles. I loved being here and feeling included in this extended family. I loved the lively conversations and the fast-paced comings and goings. It was so different from my everyday life at home.

Peter and I had found a new path to walk down. It wasn't what I'd dreamed about. But it was okay. It felt good to move along on the "friend" path with so much ease. It was much better than ousting myself from this group.

Tomorrow I'd get to experience a day in London with these lovely women and a round of sightseeing with Peter. Plus, I had the promise of getting my Christmas wish of meeting Ben face-to-face.

I watched Peter as he cleared the remaining tables and leaned over to give one of the older women a good-bye kiss on the cheek.

I pressed my lips together. The eternally hopeless romantic in me wondered, *Would it be wrong to still hope for one more Christmas wish?*

Chapter Eight

The next morning Ellie, Miranda, Julia, and I arrived at the train station just as the rumbling clouds overhead began dousing the countryside with a chilling winter rain. We got on board and peeled back our wet coats before taking our seats. We tucked our collapsed umbrellas under our seats and settled in, facing each other across a table. The windows were steamed over from all the warmth emanating from our compartment.

I felt as if we were on a grand adventure. I don't think there is a train system in the Midwest that comes close to the British railway system. Even though the inside of the train was modern, the experience of dashing to the station and feeling the sensation of rolling down the tracks made it seem as romantic as if we were in a movie from the Victorian era.

I thought about the fact that Peter and Ian both worked for the same architecture company in downtown London. "Do Ian and Peter take the train into work every day?"

"Ian does," Miranda said. "I think Peter does, too. I'm not sure. I've never asked them. Would you like something to drink? This train has a snack bar."

"Some tea would be nice."

Miranda scooted into the narrow aisle. "Ellie? Julia? Would either of you like something?"

"Nothing for me," Ellie said with a smile. "Julia, I brought along a juice box for you, if you're thirsty."

Julia had pulled out a coloring book and was busy giving a princess on the first page a blue-colored gown. She wasn't interested in the juice yet.

Miranda gently touched my shoulder. "Would you like to come with me?"

"Sure." I slid out and followed Miranda from our car through two other cars before we entered a crowded café car that had a line of people waiting to get up to the small snack bar window.

"Let's sit here and wait for the line to get shorter." Miranda slid onto a narrow bench and I squeezed in next to her.

"I was wondering," Miranda said in a low voice. "Did it seem as if Peter was less talkative with you than he'd been at our wedding?"

Miranda's gleaming eyes seemed to be searching my expression for clues as to what was going on. I didn't know what she'd seen at the wedding reception and I had no idea what Peter may have said to her or to Ian about me.

Part of me wanted to lean in like schoolgirls at lunchtime and tell her all about my elevated dreams, Peter's crushing explanation of our kiss, and how we had restarted yesterday as "friends."

But I wasn't used to talking about feelings like this with anyone, so the answer that came out was vague. "He and I had a chance to talk outside last night. It was a good talk."

"That's good."

I nodded but didn't say anything more. I liked Miranda very much and I had no reason not to believe that I could trust her. But there was a familiar voice in the back of my head that I had listened to since childhood. It was the voice of "Prudence." Prudence had kept me nestled in my padded, safe cocoon for many years. She reminded me that once a secret is shared, it's no longer a secret. And if it's no longer a secret, it's no longer yours alone.

Sitting beside Miranda on this rainy morning in the swaying club car on our way to London, I felt my timid temperament rising to the surface. It seemed best to keep all my secret Christmas wishes about Peter to myself.

When I didn't provide any further information, Miranda honored my silence. She moved on to the facts that were common knowledge. "I'm glad that Peter volunteered to show you around London today. Is there anything you're especially interested in seeing?"

"Big Ben. And maybe Saint Paul's Cathedral. What are your favorite places? What do you recommend I see?"

"There's so much. It depends on what you like. I enjoy the museums but I'm not sure how many of them will be open this evening. The V&A is one of my favorites—that is, the Victoria and Albert Museum. Both of the Tate Museums are wonderful. You have to see the front gate of Buckingham Palace, of course. And the Tower Bridge is always a favorite."

"What do you think about the London Eye?"

Miranda thought for a moment. "Do you have any aversion to heights?"

"Not particularly."

"I don't either but it's still pretty unnerving. It's so high and the enclosures you ride in made me feel uneasy. I wanted something to hold on to. I only went on it once. Ian took me when I first moved here. It's not my favorite thing but if Peter wants to take you, I suppose it's sort of an initiation to welcome you to London."

The line had shortened, so Miranda stood and motioned for me to join her.

"I have a feeling you'll like whatever he takes you to see," she said. "The Christmas decorations make everything in the city look especially beautiful."

We ordered tea and carried the corrugated paper cups back to our seats. I was grateful that the lid was nice and tight because otherwise I most likely would have had a spill. We slid in across from Julia and Ellie and admired the progress Julia had made in her coloring book.

"It's not as neat as I'd like it to be," Julia said with a sigh. "It's difficult to be neat when this train keeps being so jiggly."

I took in the views of the countryside through the rain-streaked windows, sipped my tea, and enjoyed Julia's happy chatter about every princess in her coloring book. She knew them all by name and each of them had a story.

When we arrived at Paddington Station, Julia held my hand as we tried to keep up with woman-on-a-mission Ellie. She got us into the queue outside at the taxi stand and I noticed the rain had stopped. I was grateful for that. It was still bone-chillingly cold and damp. I could feel the sharp breeze bringing icicle-like tears to my eyes.

"I never guessed England could be so cold."

Elli was wrapped up to her nose in a blue-and-white snowflake scarf. "That's saying something, coming from you. I have always imagined that there's nothing but ice and snow in places like Minnesota. I think that's because those are the only pictures they run on the news here. Whenever you break a new record for the windchill factor, our local weather reporter is eager to make it a top story."

We were next in line for the taxi. A classic, big black British taxi rolled up and we got inside. Julia bounded in first. Her rosy-cheeked face showed that she was as excited about taking a London taxicab ride as I was. We turned to look right and left as we passed rows of lovely, tall white buildings and went through a roundabout with a towering statue.

"There it is!" Julia announced. "We're almost there!"

We'd turned a corner and were pulling up to the front of Harrods. The impressive building was a city block long and trimmed with white lights, making the huge square building look like a giant gift box. I could only imagine how stunning it would look when it was lit up at night.

"It's best if we stick together," Ellie warned right before we exited the taxi. "I've gotten myself lost in this place before. Are we ready?"

We clumped together like a cluster of grapes in the midst of a well-kept vineyard. The throngs of determined shoppers seemed to give off a low hum of polite frenzy. It was as if everyone within a hundred miles of London woke up that morning and realized that Christmas was only four days away.

Once again Julia held my hand and Ellie led the charge. The elegance and beauty of every display took my breath away. The ceilings were ornately decorated and vastly different in style and design in every department. I'd never seen a store like this. The opulence of the Victorian era still reigned at Harrods.

The iconic department store was enormous but well organized. It wasn't difficult to find our way to all the various departments on Ellie's list.

My favorite department was the stationery section. Miranda purchased an expensive pen for Ian. Julia used her own money to buy a small wax and seal set for her brother with the initial *M*.

I lingered over a set of watercolors in a beautiful leather case. It seemed like the perfect souvenir but I couldn't convince myself that I needed to buy it. I had long been an avid fan of Beatrix Potter and loved all her endearing, watercolored storybook characters. Jemima Puddle-duck and Peter Rabbit were my childhood favorites.

Running my fingers over the smooth leather case, I remembered the first time I tried to copy Beatrix's beloved Peter Rabbit, for the Lake Minnetonka Junior Artists contest. I was nine and won first place. I still had the ribbon.

To her credit, my practical mother enrolled me in art classes and took me to the Minneapolis Institute of Art for lectures on Monet's haystack paintings while I was still in grade school. She sought out opportunities for me to excel and I kept improving. My favorite project up until now was a book about a village of hedgehogs that lived in pastel-colored cottages and wore tweed suits and hats made out of buttons.

Through my drawings over the years, my romantic imagination had blossomed. I put my whole heart into every sketch I did. I loved the process of filling in the carefully curved lines with watercolors.

I smiled. No one knew about the secret gift I'd brought with me for Christmas. It was a children's book for Peter's young sister titled *Molly the Little Lamb*. I almost didn't bring it with me but now I was glad I did.

My only regret was that I didn't have a second book I could slide under the Whitcombe Christmas tree titled *Julia the Lovely Princess*.

I looked at the luscious watercolors one more time and felt the anxious hum of the other shoppers vibrating inside me now. How quickly could I draw and paint a picture of "Julia the Lovely Princess"? I clutched the set of watercolors and then stopped.

Better yet, what if I sketched the pictures in a notebook and Julia could color the drawings herself?

"Ready to move on?" Ellie asked. "I think it's the Christmas room for us next. We need to hunt down a few specific ornaments."

"I need to get one more thing." I put down the leather box of watercolors and headed for the back wall to the impressive assortment of notebooks and journals. Julia followed me.

"Which one of these do you think I should get?" I asked her.

"I like this one."

"So do I." I picked up the very girly purple journal with blue flowers and headed for the cash register, smiling all the way.

Chapter Nine

$\mathcal{A}$fter spending over half an hour prowling around every corner of the Christmas room, which provided an eye-popping array of decorations, we made our purchases and found our way to the ornate Georgian Restaurant for our much-anticipated afternoon tea.

All of us, including Julia, had bought ornaments in the Christmas room and were talking about them as we were seated at a round table. I said that the cute little teapot ornament I got reminded me of the sign that hung on the lamppost by the Tea Cosy and that it would always bring me a happy memory.

"It can also bring you a happy memory of our tea party right now," Julia said enthusiastically. She scooted in her chair, getting comfortable.

"You're right. I'm sure it will. I've never been in a tearoom like this before."

"The décor used to be all pink," Ellie said. "Ever so pink. I like this look much better."

I glanced around at the gorgeous art deco style. Live palms and brass light fixtures added to the lush feeling of the burgundy-colored upholstery. I thought the design looked decadent in an almost-but-not-quite-over-the-top sort of way. The intricate Christmas decorations added a festive feeling.

"What type of tea should we have?" Ellie asked. "They've quite an assortment."

The four of us studied the menu, reviewing the tea selections and reading the descriptions of the tea along with the details on where it had been grown. I selected the No. 16 Afternoon Special Blend for my tea. That was because Julia had whispered that we should have the same kind of tea and No. 16 Afternoon Special Blend was her "favorite" because it had the word *special* in the name.

Waiters in their formal attire soon delivered four individual teapots and poured the celebrated beverage for us into our china cups. The tea was loose tea, so they used silver strainers that were then placed in silver holders. We each had our own cream and sugar accoutrements. I added a splash of milk to the dark brew and took a cautious sip.

"Mmmm."

"You sound like you're purring," Julia said politely. She sat up straight and added a spoonful of sugar and a generous amount of milk after the waiter poured only a half a cup of tea into hers. She took a sip, holding her cup with both hands, and imitated my purr of approval.

Ellie drew in a lingering sniff of her Jasmine Dragon Pearl Tea. "I must take some of this tea home with me. It's so reviving."

A three-tiered assortment of bite-sized tea treats was delivered to the table and we all listened closely as the waiter described the freshly baked pastry sweets on the top tier. Small, puffy scones occupied the middle tier and an assortment of finger sandwiches filled the lowest tier.

Julia and Ellie reached for the scones first.

"Still warm," Ellie chirped. "Lovely. Scones are always best when they're still warm. You must try the rose-petal jelly with the clotted cream. It's heavenly."

"I like mine with both the strawberry jam and the lemon curd." Julia sounded like a little connoisseur of all things fancy as she expertly opened her biscuit-like scone and swirled the strawberry jam on the outside and decorated the center with the lemon curd.

"I think I've become a purist." Miranda balanced half of a scone between her fingers and demonstrated how she had added a single dollop of the thick clotted cream to the center. It looked like a pointed ski cap. "I like to work my way to the center for the prize. But you really should try it all, Anna. That way you can decide what you like best."

I followed the advice of my experienced hostesses and was not disappointed. The soft scone crumbled on my lips. The thick, sweet clotted cream and dab of rose-petal jelly turned the first bite into a mouthful of melting deliciousness. I took a sip of my dark tea and as the flavors combined and slowly coursed down my throat, I closed my eyes and smiled.

Now this is a tea party.

The few tea parties I'd experienced in my life were at occasional baby showers or church benefits. They had never tasted anything like this. I was now a lifetime fan of having tea with friends. Especially when it was done properly.

I thought about the cute little teapot I'd just bought and realized why the ornament felt like a treasure. It was the first ornament I'd ever purchased for myself. All the other Christmas ornaments I had helped hang on the tree over the years had been my mother's ornaments. A few were my grandmother's. Each one carried a special memory. But this teapot was my very first ornament and it was infused with memories that were mine alone. I was creating my own Christmas traditions and shaping my own memories of Christmas present as well as Christmas yet to come.

The surprising thing about our sumptuous treats was how full we all became from such small portions. Everything was delicious and so of course I wanted to try everything that was offered. The sweetness lingered in my mouth and I felt immensely content.

Miranda leaned back, looking equally content. "What shall we talk about now?"

We'd already discussed our favorite Christmases, our favorite Christmas presents, and our favorite Christmas carols. Julia had a new idea for us.

"Let's talk about what we would do if we were a princess for a day."

"All right," Miranda said. "You go first, Julia."

She wiggled in her posh chair as if she'd already given this much thought and was so glad someone had finally asked her.

"I would come to London and ride around in a taxi all day

long. Whenever I wanted to stop and look at something, I would say, 'Stop here, driver.'" She put up her hand and used such a cute *Downton Abbey*, upper-class voice, we all started laughing.

"He would stop and I would roll down the window and take pictures of all my favorite places before saying, 'Drive on.'"

"That sounds like a very fun day," Ellie said. "What would you wear?"

"I would wear a blue princess gown with long strings of pearls and a tiara, of course."

"Of course," I said.

"The tiara is the most important part," Miranda said.

"Oh! And I would drink No. 16 Special Afternoon Tea all day long with milk and sugar and I would eat as many pink macaroons as my tummy would hold." Julia patted her middle and giggled.

We giggled with her. My imagination was popping with ideas for sketches to put in Julia's customized purple princess coloring journal. I couldn't wait to draw Princess Julia wearing her tiara and nibbling her pink macaroons in the long backseat of a big, black London taxi.

"Look!" Julia said, pointing behind me. "It's Peter. What is Peter doing here?"

Instead of turning around to watch him approach our table, I leaned closer to Julia and said, "He's taking me around London so I can see some of the sights."

"In a taxi?" Julia's expression was a burst of elation.

"I don't know. Maybe."

"May we come, too?" Julia asked, looking up at Peter, who was now standing by my chair.

"Not this time," Ellie answered quickly so that I didn't have to. "We need to get home with all these gifts. You're the best gift wrapper I know, Julia. You wouldn't desert me in my time of gift-wrapping need, would you?"

I turned my head and smiled up at Peter. He smiled back, looking nice in his navy blue peacoat with a Christmassy red wool scarf around his neck.

"Maybe next time, Princess Julia," I whispered before getting up.

Peter pulled out my chair for me and I tried to go through the motions as gracefully as possible. I reached down to get my purse and Julia whispered, "I wish you had a tiara you could wear."

I kissed the tip of my finger and touched the kiss to the top of her nose. I didn't need a tiara. Or pearls. Or a flowing blue gown or any pink macaroons. I had everything I'd dreamed of during the months I'd thought about this return trip to England.

Of course, my dreams of how it would be when I got to spend time with Peter had been conjured up with a much more vividly romantic imagination. Just like Julia, the little girl princess in me had imagined a storybook full of fanciful scenarios. But at that moment it didn't matter that Peter was escorting me as a "just friends" sort of tour guide. This real-life scenario was almost as thrilling as anything I'd dreamed up.

Just then, Peter gently placed his hand on the small of my back in order to steer me through the Georgian Restaurant like a gentleman. I felt like Cinderella while she still had both shoes on.

"So you want to see that old clock you keep talking about?" Peter teased.

"Yes. I just don't want it to strike midnight."

"What did you say?"

"Nothing."

Chapter Ten

*P*eter ushered me through the maze of shoppers. The crowd down on the first floor had changed to a more anxious-looking bunch. It seemed as if many of them had popped in on their way home from work. The collective hum in each department was rising.

"Did you work today?" I asked, not sure if Peter could hear me in the swirl of voices as we walked side by side, smooshed together in the crowded rooms.

"Yes. Today was my last day before the week off. It was a full day."

"I appreciate you taking the time to do this."

"Of course. It's my pleasure. I was looking forward to it."

"So was I."

"How was your tea?" he asked.

"So good! I've never had tea like that before. It was so filling."

Peter glanced at me. "You're not hungry, then?"

"No. Not at all."

"I'd thought you might want to have a bite after I take you to see your big crush."

"My big crush, huh?" I smiled at him. It was getting too noisy to talk anymore.

We exited into the cold air. I had been carrying my coat and quickly put it on. I looked up and saw that the lights were lit around the top of Harrods. "Oh, look. It's so pretty."

Peter reached for my hand and pulled me along before I could get sidetracked and caught up in the crush of people coming and going and waiting for taxis.

"This way." Peter kept hold of my hand for several blocks. I didn't mind. His hand was warm and felt rough compared to my delicate artist hand. I wondered what he was thinking. Was this a friend-to-friend hand-holding sort of thing just so I wouldn't get lost? Or did he feel like I did, that holding hands was just about the best thing to do when all the buildings around us were lighting up with Christmas lights as twilight fell on London?

He let go when we entered an Underground station. With patience, he showed me how to buy a ticket at the machine, put it in the turnstile, and then take the escalator down into the belly of London's efficient transportation system.

I was in awe at all of it. The immenseness of the tunnels, the musicians playing in the tiled corridors, the billboards, and the sound of the train approaching. The doors opened and he ushered me inside past lots of people and into the center area where we held on to a pole together with our hands just barely touching.

"I'm not jealous, mind you."

"Jealous?" I was looking directly into Peter's pale blue eyes. He was so close. I had no idea what he was talking about, though.

"In fact, he should be jealous of me."

"Who?"

"Your big crush. Ben."

I chuckled. "And why should he be jealous of you?"

"Because he's stuck. He can't leave Parliament. Not even for the holidays."

I gave Peter a funny look and then realized he was trying to make a joke. "Did you work on that joke all day?"

"No. Just on the way to the Tube. What do you think? Needs more work?"

I nodded.

"An honest critic. That's refreshing. Here. This is our stop."

I followed Peter up a long flight of stairs, warming and feeling the stretch in my legs. We emerged from the Underground and stepped out into the darkened night. The view took my breath away. A huge lion statue rested near the entrance to Westminster Bridge. Across the bridge with its Victorian-style, multiarmed streetlamps was the immense Parliament building. It stretched along the bank of the Thames River with all the windows lit and twinkling like gold coins about to be tossed into the water below.

At the end of Parliament stood Ben. Tall, stately, distinguished Big Ben, with his face glowing and his hands outstretched.

I didn't want Peter to see that I was crying. It was just a few tears and they were happy tears. I had tried my best to persuade my mother that we should come to London after the wedding last May. We had an extra day when we could have gone. Ellie had provided us with the train schedule and a link to a few helpful websites. My mother was convinced that we needed someone to go with us. She was afraid of what might happen if we tried to navigate such a monstrous city on our own. I discovered then that my mother was afraid of many things. Most of the choices she had projected onto me over the years had come from that well of fear that had been dug deep into the core of her heart.

I suppose the tears were mostly for her. She was missing this. She had tried to keep me from experiencing this splendid beauty. Why didn't she understand that this was what fed the artist in me? Moments like this fueled my passion for artistic expression. I felt alive.

Peter and I stood side by side with our hands in our pockets, gazing at what I said looked like a life-sized vintage-style mural from a Peter Pan book.

"Can't you just picture Wendy and her little brothers flying past the face of the golden clock at any moment, led by the fearless Peter?"

The real-life Peter tilted his head as if trying to imagine it. "No." He seemed fascinated that I would say such a thing.

It didn't matter that his whimsy dial wasn't turned all the way up as mine was. This was the city where he worked. All this had to be blasé and familiar to him. I drew it in, feeling the cool air as it came in through my nostrils, laced with the scent of murky riverbank and exhaust from the red double-decker buses that were passing each other on the bridge.

"Right, then." Peter clapped his hands together. "What's next on your list?"

"You're not ready to go, are you?" I looked at him in disbelief, my mouth open.

A wily sort of grin moved up from the corner of his mouth to his eyes. He playfully tagged my arm with his elbow. "I'm only teasing. Come on. I brought you up from the Tube on this side so you could have the experience of crossing the bridge. I know you're going to think he's watching you the whole time but he's not. Just so you know."

We headed for the sidewalk that lined the Westminster Bridge, walking in step. I wanted Peter to hold my hand again but I was keeping both of them warm in my pockets and he was doing the same with his hands. Besides, holding hands now would clearly be a romantic gesture whereas before it had been more of a safety precaution on the crowded sidewalk outside of Harrods.

"I wonder how old he is?" My gaze was fixed on Big Ben as we got closer and closer. Cars and buses and taxis drove past us in the center of the bridge. Hordes of people lined both sides, pausing to take pictures.

"I happen to know the answer to that. Or at least a general answer. Would you like to hear about the tower from an architect's perspective? Or will that ruin the mystique for you?"

"I think I can handle the reality. Go ahead. Tell me the cold, hard facts."

"They're rather interesting facts, I think. The clock tower was originally built in the late 1850s. Charles Barry was the chief architect. What's interesting is that he chose to go with brickwork and limestone for the base. The rest of the tower is cast iron."

Peter took his hands out of his pockets and became animated as he described the foundation that was set on a fifty-foot square raft made of concrete that was ten feet thick. He said all this in meters and then translated the amounts for me.

"They set it at a depth of four meters below ground level. That's thirteen feet down. In the last one hundred and sixty some years the structure has begun to lean slightly to the northwest. Only a couple hundred millimeters. Less than ten inches. Not bad."

I watched him fix an appreciative gaze on the tower as if he had X-ray vision and was venerating all the fine cast-iron work that none of the rest of us pedestrians could see. Peter turned to me with a look of deep admiration that fled as soon as he saw my face.

"I've ruined it for you, haven't I?"

"No," I said slowly. "I need healthy doses of reality in my life. Thank you for that."

"Can you handle one more brutal truth?"

I nodded even though I would have been fine without hearing about another meter of cement or limestone.

"Big Ben is only a nickname for the bell in the clock. It probably came from Sir Benjamin Hall who oversaw the installation of the first bell. The tower is actually the Elizabeth Tower. They renamed it not long ago in 2012 in honor of the queen's diamond jubilee. Before that it was just called Clock Tower."

I didn't say anything.

"Not another word from me," Peter said. "I've completely obliterated all your fairy-tale images now, haven't I?"

I thought for a moment, looking up into the golden face of the iconic clock. When I narrowed my eyes, I could still imagine Peter Pan soaring past it with a feather in his felt cap.

Turning to look at the human Peter beside me with his red scarf tucked around his neck and the collar of his peacoat pulled up, I calmly shook my head.

"No. You didn't change anything for me."

I still believed in fairy tales and I was pretty sure I always would.

Chapter Eleven

*T*he rest of my tour around London turned into a comfort-able blend of fantasy and reality. It was one of the best evenings of my life.

We walked to Westminster Cathedral, which wasn't far, and then ducked into a nearby pub when it started to rain again. Peter was famished and suggested we share a basket of fish and chips since I was still full from tea and I had promised him that all I'd eat was one bite. In the end I had three bites but that was all I could manage.

From there a taxi took us past Buckingham Palace where Peter explained the importance of the neoclassical style of architecture. He explained that John Nash, the architect who was largely responsible for the design of Buckingham Palace, had influenced those who followed him when they designed the Parliament building after the great fire at the Palace of Westminster in the 1830s.

"You certainly have an impressive knowledge of British history," I said as the taxi inched past St. James's Park. It was cozy in the back of the cab. The single bench seat was wide enough that we could turn and face each other as we talked.

Peter laughed at my comment. "The truth is I scored terrible marks in history. I only know about the history of the buildings and the architects I'm most interested in. You've heard the extent of my repertoire, I'm afraid."

"Who is your favorite architect?"

"John Nash. No doubt."

"He's the one who you said designed Buckingham Palace?"

"Yes. He was largely responsible. There were others, of course. His best design, in my opinion, is the Royal Pavilion at Brighton. He designed something completely different when he pulled off Indo-Saracenic style with great success."

I kept listening, and Peter kept talking, describing the rounded dome that was influenced by Britain's fascination with India during that time.

"I was seventeen when I first visited Brighton on a school trip. When I saw the Royal Pavilion, I couldn't believe anything like it existed in England. It's magnificent. If you see it at dusk, you'll think you've been transported to another world."

"So that's your big crush, then, isn't it? Little Miss Royal Pavilion."

Peter looked surprised and then seemed to catch my joke. "Yes, I suppose it is."

I looked out the rain-streaked window at the blur of lights and buildings as we drove through a wide intersection.

"I suppose you're scheming right now," Peter said. "Trying to find a way to ruin the Pavilion for me the way I ruined Big Ben for you."

"Oh, no. I would never be that cruel to anyone." I grinned. "I believe in letting people hold on to all the pleasant thoughts they have on any subject that brings them joy. There's too much else in this world that tears our hearts to pieces. We have to hold on to whatever is good and lovely and brings us hope and happiness."

He grinned.

"Besides," I added. "I know nothing about the Royal Pavilion, so I'm at a disadvantage in finding a way to diminish the enchantment you feel for her."

I liked the way Peter was looking at me. I liked the way it was easy to talk with him and the way I felt so comfortable walking with him and sitting beside him. For a moment I reminded myself of all the guard-your-heart declarations I'd made right after he'd explained that our kiss at the wedding was an accident. I thought about how he'd asked at the Tea Cosy if we could have a fresh start as friends and I had agreed.

We're friends. This is how friends spend an evening together. Don't spoil it with unrealistic romantic notions.

"What about you?" Peter asked.

"What about me?"

"What artists do you admire?"

"Beatrix Potter."

"I've been to her house in the Lake District," Peter said matter-of-factly.

"You have?"

"It's a museum, run by the National Trust. It's called Hill Top. It's not open until the spring but you should go for a tour."

"I'd love to do that."

"You could paint the wildflowers and birds. They have plenty of both in the spring around Windermere Lake."

I had no difficulty conjuring up a fanciful image of a field of quivering stalks of foxgloves and hollyhocks. I could picture all the pastel, bell-shaped flowers being used as vacation condos for visiting bees and ladybugs. With unguarded enthusiasm, I spilled out my idea for a series of watercolor pictures. "I'd add loads of ladybugs," I said. "I like drawing ladybugs."

Peter tilted his head and looked at me with the tenderest grin. "Who are you? You aren't like anyone I've ever known. And I'm not just saying that because you're an American."

My lips automatically pressed together. I wasn't sure if I'd said too much.

"You're a bit of a fairy tale, aren't you?"

His comment caught me off guard. I didn't know how to answer. The comment seemed to catch him off guard as well.

Peter straightened up and said, "I'll tell you something I don't tell many people." He glanced at me cautiously and then turned to look out the cab window. "I didn't like Beatrix Potter when I was a child."

"Then why did you go to her house?"

"I was on a bike race that went through that area. The Fred Whitton Challenge. It's held every year."

"So you stopped in the middle of a bike race and went on a tour of the home of an artist you never liked."

"I didn't like her because of one reason."

"What's that?"

"Peter Rabbit," he said with a flat expression. "It's a terrible childhood nickname."

"I love Peter Rabbit! I won a contest for a drawing I did of Peter Rabbit when I was little. But I can see why being called Peter Rabbit would be a negative for you. What about Peter Pan?"

"Peter Pan?" he repeated.

"Did you grow up being called Peter Pan as well?"

"No, I was never called Peter Pan. Not sure why. Maybe because it's not as sissy sounding as Peter Rabbit. What about you?"

I leaned back. "No. I was never called Peter Pan, either. Or Peter Rabbit."

Peter laughed.

I liked that he thought I was humorous. My style of silliness had rarely met with much of a response at home. Occasionally my father would give me a nod or a meager smile when I said something I thought was witty. My mother never seemed to get my jokes and so most of them went unshared. It was fun to say whatever came to mind when I was with Peter.

"You like to ride bikes a lot, don't you?" My thoughts had returned to the image of him participating in a bike race.

"Yes, I do. I have a route around Carlton Heath that I like to take in the early mornings. It's a gorgeous ride. You'd like it."

"Then I'll have to go on a gorgeous ride with you sometime."

Peter pulled back slightly, as if he didn't want his suggestion to sound like an invitation to a date. "What about you?" he said, returning to the previous topic. "What horrible nicknames were you called when you were young?"

I thought a moment. "I was called Anna Banana at school sometimes but I didn't mind because it came from my closest friends."

"Sounds like you had a pretty docile childhood, then. No school yard bullies."

"No, no school yard bullies. I had a pretty idyllic childhood." I went ahead and stated the most accurate description of my life, in case he hadn't guessed it yet. "I've had a pretty sheltered life. What about you?"

"Mine was a mix, I guess you could say. I'm on solid ground now." He leaned forward and said to the driver, "You can let us off up here. Wherever it's convenient to stop. We're headed to Saint Martin-in-the-Fields. Close to the front portico, if possible."

We got out on the slippery, wet pavement and made our way through a cluster of people until we were in front of the steps that led to the door of a stately looking church. I knew it wasn't St. Paul's. It wasn't grand enough. This church had pillars that held up a wide portico and an uncomplicated façade. A gloriously lit-up, multitiered steeple rose behind from the back of the church. I climbed the steps with Peter and stopped when he did. There were people everywhere and I could hear carolers in the distance.

"Turn around," he said. "I thought you'd like to see this."

We were facing Trafalgar Square. The huge fountain was immersed in white lights and flowing joyously. A large choir was assembled on risers and I caught the words, "The stars are brightly shining; it is the night of our dear Savior's birth."

Between us and the fountain was the largest Christmas tree I'd ever seen. It towered into the night sky and was lit with yards and yards of vivid lights trailing from the brilliant star on top down to the base.

"Norway sends us her best every year," Peter said. "It's an ongoing gift of appreciation for our help during World War II."

I couldn't find any words to comment on the magnificent beauty of the enormous spruce tree and all the lights and color and swarms of people that had gathered. It was all of the best that can happen in a big city at Christmastime. Publicly sung praises to God, hundreds and hundreds of people with smiles on their faces as they gazed at the lights and hummed along with the Christmas carols. It was peace on earth. It was a gathering of goodwill toward men.

I felt overwhelmed with the joy of the moment and slipped my arm through Peter's. I rested my head on his shoulder, but only for a moment. It was my innocent way of saying thank you without formulating any words. Such a gift as this required a heartfelt acknowledgment.

He gave my arm a squeeze and I retracted, slipping my hand back in my pocket. Peter kept looking straight ahead, listening to the carols. I hoped he'd read my message correctly and that my sudden cozy expression hadn't seemed too forward.

A moment later, Peter quietly reached over and pulled my hand from out of my coat pocket. He threaded my arm through his arm once again and slipped my cold hand into his warm coat pocket. His hand clasped mine inside his pocket and he gave me a squeeze. I bravely squeezed back, not sure what this sweet but clearly affectionate gesture was supposed to mean.

Prudence told me to withdraw. Pull back. Don't be so easily wooed. Be on your guard.

I thought and thought and thought some more.

And then I told Prudence she didn't have to worry. I knew what I was doing. Everything was as it should be on a night like this and at a moment like this.

The choir sang out, "O ni-i-ght divine, O-o-o night, when Christ was born. O night divine! O-o night, O night divine."

I was holding my breath on the powerful final note. As soon as the carol came to a triumphant end, Peter and I let go and freed our hands so that we could join the throng around us and offer a wild applause. Such perfection deserved immediate recognition.

It turned out that was the final song. The crowd dispersed. Peter and I didn't end up navigating back into any sort of naturally occurring hand-holding during the rest of our evening tour of London. I saw that as proof that Prudence didn't need to worry about a thing.

The connection had been for that moment and that moment only. It seemed as if we'd both needed a way to express our shared appreciation for the experience we'd stumbled upon. I couldn't help but wonder, though, if he was thinking what I was thinking.

Holding hands was lovely.

The gesture warmed more than my hand. It warmed my heart.

Peter and I found lots to talk about but I was having difficulty staying awake on our trek home. We traveled first by Tube to the train station and then took a somber train ride to Carlton Heath. We rode in a packed train car filled with shoppers and travelers and generally weary folks.

I leaned my head on the closed window and fell asleep within a few minutes. Jet lag had at last caught up with me. Peter was sitting across from me rather than next to me, due to the crowded conditions. He had to rouse me when we arrived at the station.

"Anna. We're here."

I looked up, touching the back of my hand to the side of my mouth and hoping I hadn't drooled while I slept.

Peter's rather rusty old-model car was parked at the station. He drove me back to Whitcombe Manor with the heater at full blast. I tried to come around and wake up enough to express to him how much I'd enjoyed the tour and how wonderful it had all been.

"It was great," he agreed. "I especially liked hearing what you said when you talked in your sleep on the train ride."

My eyes were instantly opened all the way. It was impossible to read his expression in the darkened car to tell if he was teasing me. He punched in the code to the front gate at Whitcombe Manor and drove to the front entrance.

"What did I say?" I asked cautiously.

Peter turned off the motor and got out. He came around and opened the door for me. The amber lights in the alcove over the front door were on, welcoming me back. The Christmas tree was gleaming in the front window.

He offered me a hand. I got out and he let go.

Adjusting my shopping bags and looping my purse over my shoulder, I faced him and asked again. "What did I say on the train?"

Peter grinned. "I'll never tell."

He leaned in. Now that I recognized the signs for the proper good-bye kiss procedure, I turned my cheek at the right moment but turned too far. His whisper of a kiss landed just behind my ear.

He paused as if trying to decide if he wanted to try it again with a little more grace.

"I'll see you tomorrow," he said. "At the play."

"Oh, yes. The play. I'll see you there." I felt embarrassed and could tell that my face was starting to turn rosy. "Thanks again."

"My pleasure." Peter turned and got in the driver's seat.

I waved as he drove off. Instead of going inside right away, I stared up into the night sky. The rain clouds had cleared and a dozen faithful stars glistened in the inky heavens.

"O, holy night," I sang softly. "The stars are brightly shining..."

I drew in a deep breath of the chilly air and entered Whitcombe Manor under the motto GRACE AND PEACE RESIDE HERE.

Just as I stepped inside, the grandfather clock in the entry hall chimed.

One, two, three...

I counted until the last chime made twelve in all. It was midnight. I looked down, smiling at the irony of the chiming clock and silently congratulating myself for returning with both shoes.

Even without a tiara, my princess-for-a-day adventure had come to a lovely conclusion.

Best of all, I was going to see Peter again tomorrow.

Chapter Twelve

I slept in the next morning and by the time I found my way downstairs, the Whitcombe household was in a flurry of activity. Ellie was in the kitchen writing out a grocery list for everything she needed for the Christmas feast.

Julia was concentrating on adding just the right amount of sprinkles to all the cookies she and Ellie had baked that morning.

Edward had gone into town to get the programs printed and then was planning to help get everything set up at the community theater for the play that evening.

"Did you have a nice time last night?" Ellie asked. "How was your night on the town?"

"Wonderful!" I described how much I enjoyed seeing Big Ben and how we'd had fish and chips and ended up at Trafalgar for the surprising and meaningful Christmas celebration. "I can't wait to go back to London again. There's so much to see."

"I wish I could have gone with you," Julia said with a pout. "I like fish and chips."

I leaned across the counter and looked Julia in the eye. "Well, I have something to tell you, then."

She looked at me expectantly. Her innocent little face filled with Christmas hope and wonder.

"Your mom and dad have invited me to come back in the spring. Why don't you and I plan to go to London together when I come back? We'll have fish and chips and go to the art museums you were telling me about. What do you think?"

"Will Peter come with us and take us around in a taxi?"

I turned away because I felt my face beginning to turn rosy at the mention of Peter. "I guess we'll have to wait and see about that." I opened the refrigerator and helped myself to some orange juice.

"That sounds encouraging." Ellie caught my eye and raised an eyebrow. Clearly, she was hoping for additional hints on how things had really gone last night.

I felt bashful and avoided Ellie's gaze. Last spring my hopes about Peter had grown wild like an overly fed and watered rose-bush. Peter's clarification on my first day here had cut us way back to being "friends." Just friends.

When I was dressing that morning, I could hear Prudence reminding me that my severely cut-back dreams were now down to a stump. If, indeed, that stump had sprouted a hint of something more last night, then it was best to let it take its time to grow naturally. Or wither.

Either way, I wanted to return in the spring without any awkwardness.

"So," I held my glass of orange juice with both hands and looked over Julia's shoulder. "How goes the cookie-decorating project?"

"I'm nearly finished. How do you like this one?" Julia held up a star-shaped sugar cookie with an excessive amount of multicolored sprinkles.

"Beautiful."

"You can have it. Here."

I took a bite and felt all the sugar sprinkles clinging to my lips. "Mmmm. Delicious." I looked over at Ellie. "I love the flavor."

"I use almond instead of vanilla extract. Gives it that little something extra. Each year the critics become a little more vocal about the treats we serve during intermission at the play. I've had to step up my contributions."

"These will definitely be a hit."

"Miranda is baking this morning as well. She called earlier and asked if you wanted to go over and keep her company. That is, if you didn't have plans already with anyone else."

"I don't have any plans." I gave Ellie an unflinching smile, hoping it would curtail her from doing any more fishing to try to catch details about Peter. "I'd love to help her."

"All right, then. I can give you a ride over to Rose Cottage in a few minutes. Julia and I were about to do our shopping."

"Great. I'll grab my things." The main item I wanted to take with me was the purple notebook from Harrods. I had a very important Christmas gift that needed immediate attention. I loaded up my large shoulder bag with all my art supplies and grabbed my coat and scarf.

By the time I'd returned downstairs, Ellie had efficiently packed up the finished cookies, put away the washed cookie sheets, and had Julia bundled up and ready to go.

"I certainly wasn't much help this morning," I said on our short drive to Miranda and Ian's.

Ellie brushed off my sort-of apology. "You'll have plenty to do in helping Miranda."

Their quaint little cottage had belonged to Sir James and was tucked away in an idyllic setting. I had begun a sketch of Rose Cottage on the morning after Ian and Miranda's wedding but hadn't finished it. That was the morning when I saw Peter riding his bike with Molly. She was riding in her special wagon-like seat that he'd affixed on the front. I remembered being touched by the way he treated her with such patience and kindness.

I waved good-bye to Julia and sauntered up the path to the front door. It was decorated with a beautiful wreath that appeared to be crafted from fresh greenery and dried wildflowers. I knocked and heard Miranda call out, "Come in!"

I stepped inside and all my artistic senses were filled with a rush of Christmas beauty and joy. Amber flames danced in the fireplace. A thick garland of greens dotted with red berries lined the mantel. The inviting fragrance of gingerbread mixed with the scent of the fresh greenery caused me to stop where I was and draw in a deep breath. Christmas carols played in the background. The windowsills were decorated with ivory candles and in the center of the small dining table was a beautiful, old-world style nativity scene.

The tree was lit with white twinkling lights and the branches were adorned with deep red roses along with a simple collection of ornaments. Crowning the top of the tree was the delicate angel Miranda had purchased yesterday at Harrods. The angel figurine's silver-white wings were spread in a protective pose over the tree and, it seemed, over this blessed cottage.

"Miranda!"

She stood in the tiny kitchen space that was open to the rest of the living area. She had oven mitts on both hands and was wearing a cute red-and-white Christmas apron covering her jeans and T-shirt. Her smile was contagious. "Merry Christmas! I'm so glad you came over."

I motioned to the stunning décor all around me. "Miranda, this is adorable. No, not adorable. It's extraordinary! Gorgeous! Wow! I feel like I just walked into a magazine picture of Christmas perfection."

"I love Christmas. I never had any of this while I was growing up, so all of this is new to me and I can't stop myself. You'll have to see what I did in the bathroom. Ian started calling me a 'Christmas-crazed American.'"

I put down my shoulder bag brimming with art supplies and took off my coat. "I'm going to check out the bathroom right now."

She pointed the way. I peeked inside and saw that Miranda had added a string of white twinkle lights to the rim of the oval mirror. The white bath towels hanging on pegs on the wall were tied with wide red ribbons with sprigs of green holly berries tucked in the bows.

Miranda joined me. "Like I said, Ian is tolerating my fancy

touches. He likes the living room a lot but decorating the 'loo,' as he calls it, seems excessive to him. I love it, though, and he says if it makes me happy, he can navigate his way around all the fluff for a few weeks."

I was studying the wall where Miranda had hung an assortment of small frames. Each one had a different antique-style image of Father Christmas wearing a white fur-trimmed robe and a long, pointed cap that folded over his shoulder.

"I found those old postcards at a bookshop in the next village over. Aren't they great? They look like the style of costumes that are worn each year for the Dickens play."

"I love these."

"I know. So do I. My favorite is the one on top. It reminds me of how Ian looked last Christmas when he wore the vintage costume for the play."

"I remember someone talking about it at your wedding. He must have made a memorable Father Christmas."

"It's a big deal here in Carlton Heath, as you have probably heard. Sir James started the tradition a long time ago. He used to play the role of Father Christmas and after he was gone, Andrew took on the role. But when Andrew was ill last year, the part fell to Ian. He was great at it. So good with all the kids." Miranda smiled.

I looked at the top picture more closely. The long white beard on the Gandalf-esque Father Christmas flowed to his waist. He was holding a small Christmas tree decorated with miniature carvings of woodland creatures. The details in the drawing were impressive. I couldn't determine the method used to draw it unless I could take it out of the frame and look at the paper more closely.

"This is an exceptional drawing," I told Miranda. "It makes me want to sketch a Father Christmas card right now. I never had much of an interest in drawing a Santa. But this would be a nice challenge."

"You're welcome to take it down or take it with you, if you want."

"No, I better finish the projects I brought with me—that is, after you let me help you with all your baking. Ellie seemed to think you were in need of some backup assistance."

Miranda chuckled. Her dark hair was pulled back with a wide red ribbon that looked like it came from the same spool as the ribbons on the towels. "I'm sure she said that because Ellie knows I'm not much of a cook or a baker. This year I'm only making goodies that I can pour into a pan and cut into small squares. The gingerbread is almost done. The brownies go in next."

"Do you need help with anything?"

"No. All the batter is mixed and ready to go for the next three batches, but my oven is too small to do more than one pan at a time. And I only have two baking pans. That's why it's going to take most of the day."

"Would you mind if I sketched while the goodies are baking?"

"Of course not! Please make yourself at home. Would you like something to drink?"

I pulled out my art supplies and thought a moment. "Not to sound too much like a Scandinavian from Minnesota, but do you happen to have any coffee? Dark coffee?"

"As a matter of fact, I do. I'm a coffee drinker, too. I like tea, but in the morning I do much better if I start with a cup of dark coffee. Is French press okay?"

"Sounds fancy, so yes. Absolutely." I settled in one of the high-back chairs by the fire and made sure I was facing the kitchen so that it would be easy to keep our conversation going while Miranda baked.

The unmistakable fragrance of deep, dark coffee wafted my direction and I smiled. It was like having the best of all worlds. A bit of home, a lot of English countryside charm, and a blossoming friendship with Miranda. I knew it was going to be excruciating to leave all this in less than a week. I closed my eyes and breathed in the moment. I didn't want to forget any of it.

Chapter Thirteen

$\mathcal{I}$'ve been meaning to tell you how glad Ian and I are that you came for Christmas." Miranda turned down the volume on the Christmas music. "I didn't realize how much I missed hearing a familiar accent and being around a fellow American. It's wonderful to have you here. I only wish you were staying longer."

I told her about Ellie's invitation and how I hoped to return in the spring. The first question she asked after that was about Peter. Unlike Ellie and her politely subtle raised eyebrow style of probing, Miranda dove right in.

"Do you think there's something there?" she asked. "I mean, you two seemed to hit it off nicely at our wedding."

"We did," I agreed cautiously. Once again Prudence was telling me to guard my secret thoughts and not entrust myself to anyone. I found it difficult to do so because I liked Miranda very much and wanted to keep our cousin connection growing even closer.

"How has it been for you to be around Peter now? Is he show-ing an interest in being more than friends?"

"No." The answer popped out before I could decide if that was the most honest assessment. "I mean, he's nice and friendly. We had a great time last night and he was a terrific tour guide. But he made it clear the first time I saw him after I arrived that he's only interested in being friends."

Miranda looked at me as if trying to decide if she wanted to believe me or not.

"We're good chums," I said a little too brightly. "I'm fine with that. I didn't come here looking for love."

I wasn't sure if I agreed with my own statement. I definitely didn't want to read in Miranda's inquisitive eyes whether she was buying it. My eyes lowered to my lap where the purple notebook was awaiting my attention.

"You know, I've wondered how it was for you when you moved here. Did you feel at home right away?"

The best thing about Miranda, I decided just then, was her calm way of understanding how to shift topics and make others feel comfortable in the midst of it. She started telling me the whole story of how she found her way into the Whitcombe fam-ily. She had come to England a couple years ago in search of her birth father, whom she'd never met. Miranda never imagined her father would be Sir James. Happenstance, as my cousin Ian had called it, led her to the Tea Cosy where she was soon enveloped into the Whitcombe family at Christmas.

"It took Edward a while before he accepted me as his half sis-ter. Now that he has, I feel at home here in every way."

Miranda slowly plunged down the stopper on her glass French press. She looked out the window and added, "Now that the paparazzi have moved on to other, more interesting women, I feel that I'm accepted by all the members of the Whitcombe family. Edward's mother, Margaret, was especially gracious to me, considering all the circumstances. You haven't met her yet and you probably won't. When Ian and I got engaged last Christmas, she announced two days later that she was going to live with her daughter in Bedford. No one could believe she'd move out of the manor, but she did. She said it was because Bedford is closer to her doctors in Cambridge. I still feel that in spite of her kindness in welcoming me into the family, she prefers to not be around me."

"Why?"

"I'm the constant reminder that her husband was unfaithful."

"But you had nothing to do with that."

"I know. But the media had a field day when they found out and security had to be hired to keep the photographers from intruding into the lives of the family. As I said, it all died down. Ian and I chose to make our home here, so I think that's why Margaret chose to make her home elsewhere."

"But you said she was kind to you and welcomed you here."

"She did. And grace offered in words can be very healing, but actions are the true expression of love. I want to believe that Margaret left Whitcombe Manor as a gesture of love to Ian and me as well as a way of finding her own sort of comfort in the face of a difficult family situation."

I nodded my understanding. "That's similar to what I've seen in my mother. She's given full-time care to her father-in-law, my Opa. He's been an invalid for almost six years now and lives at my parents' home."

I realized that all the unbending, methodical, and cautious traits I'd recently come to dislike in my mother had been the exact qualities that allowed her the strength and steady peace necessary to provide the intensive, ongoing care my Opa needed.

A burst of appreciation for my mother, just the way she was, came over me. I was the one who needed to extend more grace. More love.

Miranda brought over my requested cup of dark coffee in a Christmas mug, of course. That prompted us to slip into a less intense discussion of our favorite Christmas movies and favorite Christmas carols. She told me about the woman she lived with after her mother passed away and how the Santa Cruz cat-loving woman was fond of tofu.

"She gave me my first pair of Birkenstocks," Miranda said. "And she loved God. It was the most peculiar combination. Every morning as I ate my bowl of granola with chia seeds and acai berries, long before that combination was popular, she read to me from the Psalms."

Miranda put the pan of brownies in the oven, removed her kitchen mitts, and joined me by the fire. "Two years ago when I first came here, it felt as if God was close to me in this place. It was the first time since the granola years that I'd felt that way. I came here on a search for my birth father. But at the Christmas Eve service I felt as if I'd found my Heavenly Father."

Miranda took a sip of coffee from her snowflake-pattern mug.

"In a way, I think my Heavenly Father was the one I'd really been searching for all along."

"I came to Christ in a similar way. It was at a Christmas Eve candlelight service at my grandmother's big church in Minneapolis. I don't know what it was, exactly. The music, perhaps. Or maybe it was the profound meaning in the Scripture passages that were read during the church service. All I know is that when my grandmother turned to light my candle from hers, I whispered a childlike prayer and told Jesus I wanted to give Him my heart."

Miranda nodded as if she understood exactly.

"Have you heard the Christina Rossetti poem? The children recited it at the Christmas Eve service two years ago." Miranda reached for a small red book on the coffee table. The title was *Best Loved Christmas Poems*. The cover had a Victorian look and it fit in perfectly with Miranda's other careful design choices.

"Here it is. 'In the Bleak Midwinter.' It's the last stanza. 'What can I give Him, poor as I am? If I were a shepherd, I would bring a lamb; If I were a Wise Man, I would do my part; Yet what can I give Him: Give my heart.'"

"I love that. I've never heard it before."

"It's also a song that's popular here around Christmastime with the children's choir."

"That's exactly how I felt. I wanted to give my heart and life to God for Christmas."

Both of us seemed to find great joy in the way our conversation flowed effortlessly like spring snowmelt on a sunny Minnesota morning. I had always followed my dad's advice to never talk to anyone about religion or politics. But this didn't feel like we were talking about religion. We were talking about a relationship and the way we had each come into a loving, growing relationship with the One who became a baby on that first Christmas so long ago.

Miranda leaned back in her wingback chair. "Your powers of concentration impress me. You've been drawing the whole time we've been talking."

"I'm on a Christmas deadline. I'm making a princess coloring book for Julia."

"You are?"

I handed her the book so she could see the first two completed illustrations.

"Anna, this is so cute. Julia is going to love it." She looked over at me and gave me a look of amazement. It was the way I felt when I walked into her beautifully, artistically decorated home.

"The next one I'm going to draw is Princess Julia with her tiara in the backseat of a London taxi with stacks and stacks of pink macaroons. Well, actually, they'll be stacks of macaroons. She can color them anything she wants. Pink, green, purple."

"You are so gifted, Anna. I can't believe you haven't done more illustrations for children's books. Would you like to do more?"

I nodded. "I'm just beginning to figure out how to write and illustrate my own books and have them printed as well."

"Sounds like a huge endeavor."

"It was."

"Does that mean you've already published your own children's book?"

I hesitated. Prudence told me to keep my secret to myself. This could turn out to be quite embarrassing.

In my shoulder bag was a wrapped Christmas gift that I'd brought with me. I hadn't told anyone about it. No one had seen it yet, except for the printer in Pennsylvania that I paid in order to have three copies made. The other two copies were hidden in my room at home.

"I'm sorry. I didn't mean to sound pushy," Miranda said.

"No. I didn't take it as pushy. I hesitated because I do have a children's book that I wrote. I have it with me. It's just that I haven't shown it to anyone yet."

Miranda's eyes gave me a tender, pleading sort of look. "I would love to see it. I really would. If you don't feel comfortable showing me because it's a gift, I understand. I'll see it after you give it to Julia."

I shifted in my chair, feeling uncomfortable and yet so eager to connect with Miranda. We'd been honest and open and vulnerable in our conversation ever since I entered this cottage of comfort and joy. It seemed stingy of me to hold back from showing her the gift.

With a deep breath for courage, I told Prudence to take a hike.

Miranda will understand. And if seeing the book prompts her to ask a lot more questions, so be it.

I pulled the bubble-wrapped gift from my bag and gingerly handed it to her with my telltale confession.

"The book isn't for Julia."

Chapter Fourteen

*M*iranda received the wrapped book with a grateful look. She carefully undid the wrapping and held the book in her hands. As she studied the cover, a knowing look dawned on her. The illustration was of a sweet-faced lamb with a tiny pink triangle of a nose and very short legs.

"*Molly the Little Lamb.*" She read the title with the same conviction as she'd read the Christina Rossetti poem.

Somehow that small gesture made me feel as if she viewed my handiwork as a real book. An artistic accomplishment that deserved to be treated with honor and appreciation. It was the kind of affirmation I'd never received at home.

"You wrote this and illustrated this for Molly."

I nodded. My shyness gauge jumped ten points.

"Peter is going to be so surprised. He adores his little sister." Miranda carefully turned to the first page, smiling.

"The story is about Pete, the loyal sheepdog," I explained.

"He's responsible to herd all the little lambs in the meadow and he does so by riding his shiny bicycle around and gathering the flock."

Miranda turned the pages as I told her the story.

"Pete the loyal sheepdog gets all of the little lambs rounded up except for Molly. You see, her legs are too short for her to keep up with all the other lambs. So Pete comes up with a solution and, well, you'll see his invention there on the last page."

Miranda broke into a wide grin as she turned to the last page. "It's just like the wagon-style seat that Peter made for Molly on the front of his bike."

I nodded, feeling my nervousness dissipate. "That way Pete the sheepdog can keep Molly with him on his bike while he pedals around the pasture and herds all the other sheep."

"Anna, this is adorable. I love these darling red shoes you drew on Molly's short little legs. And the illustration of this sheepdog with all the shaggy hair flipping in front of his eyes. This is really wonderful." She closed the book and ran her fingers over the cover. "Where can I get a copy?"

I laughed.

"What's so funny?"

"That's one of three copies. I had it specially done through one of those places that can print a few books at a time."

"You need to make more. I want a copy and I'm sure Ellie and Julia will. And Andrew and Katharine. Katharine will want to sell them in the Tea Cosy. Why don't you send it to a publisher? It's so good."

I brushed off Miranda's comment. I could see lots of flaws with the book. According to the printer, I hadn't prepared the standard number of pages and the words would have been easier to read if I'd selected a different font. Plus, the watercolor illustrations should have been transferred through a different format before I sent the files in to be printed. I tried to explain all the beginner foibles to Miranda but she was undaunted in her enthusiasm.

"Seriously, Anna. This book is wonderful." She flipped through the pages again. "I love it. Peter will love it, too. And of course, Molly will be elated." Miranda carefully returned it to the bubble wrapping. "I spoiled the gift wrap, but I have lots of wrapping paper. When are you going to give it to Peter?"

"That's a good question. I was actually thinking that maybe you or Ian could slip it to Peter tonight at the play or maybe drop it by his parents' house tomorrow night, on Christmas Eve."

"Don't you want to give it to him?"

I gave a shy shrug. "I don't know. Maybe I should save it and mail it to Molly for her birthday. Do you know when her birthday is?"

"No, I don't." Miranda got up and reached for her cell phone on the counter. She started tapping a text message. "Ian and Peter are over at the theater helping Edward get everything set up for tonight. If you like, I could ask if Peter wants to stop by here when they're finished. You could give it to him then."

Just then the front door opened and Ian bounded inside.

My heart did a funny arabesque spin and landed in a flop.

Ian was alone.

"I was just going to send you a message and see how things were going."

Ian untied his boots and left them by the door. "Many hands make light work. We finished early." He sniffed the air. "Did they send me home here to the biscuit factory just in time to make sure you didn't burn the cottage down?"

"The brownies!" Miranda slipped into her mitts and opened the oven. She pulled out the pan and gave the center a spongy poke. "They look perfect. I don't know why the timer didn't go off, though. This oven is so fickle."

Ian looked my direction and seemed surprised to see me. "Oh, hallo, Anna. I thought you might still be sleeping."

"I'm not that jet-lagged."

"That's not what I heard."

"Oh, yeah? What did you hear?"

"Peter said you fell asleep on the train ride back last night."

"That's true. I did."

Ian stood at the kitchen counter, waiting for Miranda to look away before he cut himself a nice-sized piece of gingerbread.

"Ian! Those are for our family and friends and for the play tonight."

He gave her a look of mock offense. Putting on a Scottish brogue that sounded just like his father, he said, "What are you sayin', woman? Are you daft? Am I not your family? Am I not your friend? Have I not just come from doing the labor of an honest man so that you and your family and your friends might have the privilege of sitting in comfort as you enjoy the play tonight?"

Miranda was laughing before he even got to the "daft" line. She went over and wrapped her arms around Ian's middle giving him a hug with her face resting on his puffed-out chest. Her undying affection for him showed all over her face.

"That's more like it," Ian said, concluding his spot-on imitation of his father.

I'd only seen my Uncle Andrew go into one of his playful bellowing moments once before. It was at the wedding when he danced with me and couldn't contain the sheer joy of being a man who had lived to see the day that his son was married. It was the purest sort of happiness and I'd thought of that moment often whenever I felt something strongly but held back or withdrew my true feelings and replaced my reaction with a more sedate, acceptable response.

Miranda went back to the oven, still glowing. She put in the next pan of gingerbread and started getting the frosting ready. I returned to my drawing of Princess Julia in the taxi. Ian helped himself to another slice of gingerbread and came over to sit across from me by the fire.

"Peter told me something else."

"Oh?" I tried to play it coy but one of the downsides of never hanging out with the popular girls was that I'd missed out on learning how to be charming on demand.

Ian leaned back with his hands folded behind his neck. "He told me that the two of you had a divine evening together."

"Divine?" Miranda repeated from the kitchen.

Ian put up his hand in defense. "His words, not mine. Divine is what he said. Something about the Christmas tree in Trafalgar and the choir at Saint Martin-in-the-Fields."

I felt my face warming at the memory.

"Look at that," Ian said to Miranda, grinning at my reaction. "I'd say Peter wasn't the only one who would use the word *divine* to describe last night."

"It was holy," I said firmly, as if I had any possibility of changing the direction my cousin's mind had gone. "We stood on the steps of a church by the huge tree and listened to the choir sing 'O Holy Night.' It was..."

I gave up and decided it didn't matter if Ian wanted to tease me. What mattered is that Peter had told him that our time together had been "divine." That was something. I wasn't sure what, but it was something.

Ian hopped up and reached for the poker to stoke the fire. "Like I said, Peter thought you and your evening with him were both divine."

I noticed how he added the *you* to the divine comment this time but I decided to do my best to ignore Ian. It was not likely that I'd be able to discern if the added part about Peter thinking that I was divine as well had truly come from Peter's lips or if my rowdy cousin had decided to add it in to see how many shades of red he could get my face to turn.

I hoped when I saw Peter tonight at the play that I'd be able to pick up something that would give me a hint of his true feelings. The way he treated me around his family and friends in a public setting would tell me a whole lot more than any mirthful statements Ian tossed around. I didn't dare let my imagination wander off into fairy-tale land. Not without more evidence directly from Peter that he was truly interested in me as more than a friend.

Miranda's statement about Margaret flashed in my thoughts.

Grace offered in words can be very healing, but actions are the true expression of love.

Chapter Fifteen

$\mathscr{I}$ lingered at Rose Cottage for the rest of the afternoon and felt, truly, like family with Miranda and Ian.

Miranda completed her baking and frosting. I focused on finishing the coloring book and Ian kept the fire going and did his bit of sketching on a project he'd brought home from the architecture firm where he and Peter worked.

All teasing and taunting about Peter had subsided.

Twilight was coming on and Miranda had prepared a simple supper for us of pasta and salad. The three of us tucked in, as Ian liked to say, around the small kitchen table with the nativity scene taking up the center space.

"This is a beautiful set," I told Miranda. "Have you had it long?"

"No. Ellie got it for me last year at an after-Christmas sale. She loves it when she finds a bargain. She gave it to me last January because she said she was afraid if she put it away she'd forget all about it and not be able to find it again this Christmas."

Ian's phone buzzed and he glanced at it to see the text message. "It's Peter," he said.

I didn't know if I should believe him, so I kept eating as if news of Peter didn't interest me.

"Aww, that's a pity."

"What is it?" Miranda asked.

Ian scrolled down the screen on his phone. "Molly is running a fever. Peter is staying home with her tonight so that his parents can go to the play. It's the highlight of their year, he says."

"I hope Molly is all right," I said.

"She spikes fevers every now and then," Ian said. "It's usually gone by the next day. Of course, they don't want to take a chance since so many viruses are going around this time of year."

"How are your dad and Katharine?" I asked. "I've been meaning to ask."

"Katharine is over her cold. She's feeling fine. My dad never had one. He's fine."

"I thought he was sick, too, since he didn't join in the other night at the Tea Cosy."

"He was feeling all right but he and Katharine thought it best for both of them to close themselves off upstairs that evening. If he was coming down with the same cold, they didn't want to expose the entire cast of the play."

"That was a nice preemptive gesture," I said.

Ian turned to me. "If you've ever heard my dad sneeze, he can raise the roof. He could have taken out the whole cast with a single sneeze that night."

"It's too bad that Peter is going to miss tonight," Miranda said.

"Sometimes I think he's too good of a son," Ian said. "It's not my place to say that, of course."

"Why do you say that?" Miranda asked.

"I know Molly was a bit of a surprise baby—there's a big age gap between her and Peter. But I don't think if I had a sister born with special needs that I'd be as devoted as Peter is to helping care for her."

"I'm sure his parents appreciate all that he does for them. They're quite a bit older than your dad and Katharine. It has to be difficult for them." Miranda got up from the table and returned with a pitcher of water to refill my glass.

"I've no doubt they appreciate him. I'm saying as his friend that there has to come a time when he separates his life from theirs and gives himself the freedom to make decisions about his own life apart from Molly's needs. It's almost a case of Peter having too much loyalty."

I absorbed Ian's and Miranda's insights about their close friend and at the same time felt that Ian didn't understand how difficult it is to make independent decisions when you live under the same roof as someone who needs constant care.

"It's difficult with my grandfather," I said. "He's not difficult. What I mean is that it's difficult when my parents have plans to do something and I announce that I have plans for the same evening. Someone has to give in and be there for Opa. We can't leave him alone."

"You probably understand Peter's situation better than we do," Ian said.

"What is Molly's condition?" It felt odd referring to it as a "condition." When I met her last May, I realized immediately that something was off with her. It wasn't an obvious situation as with someone who has Down syndrome or something such as cerebral palsy. Molly was able to function. She wore a brace on one of her legs and she could communicate even though it didn't come out in clear or complete sentences. She was very sweet and affectionate.

Miranda looked at Ian. "I don't know—do you?"

Ian shook his head. "I know they had her tested last summer and for the second time she hadn't progressed in her intelligence. Where she's at now might be as far as she goes in that respect. All I'm saying is that it's a long time to be devoted to helping raise your little sister. Peter is a better man than most—that's for certain."

"No one at this table disagrees with you on that." Miranda looked at me with a twinkle in her eye.

Ian winked at me.

I kept my head down and finished my plate of pasta.

Chapter Sixteen

We arrived early at the community theater. Miranda and I drove together with plates of intermission goodies stacked in a large box that I balanced on my lap in the cramped sports car. Ian had caught a ride earlier with his father. He was waiting for us when we arrived and helped carry the heavy box.

The walkway to the front door was lined with lanterns hung on shepherd's hooks. The candles inside the lanterns gave a warm welcome as well as a nod to the ambience we were supposed to feel, which was that we were stepping back into Victorian times.

It seemed to me that the architectural style of the theater was well over a hundred years old but I soon noticed that it had the same sort of double doors as my high school. A plaque at the front main entrance listed May 19, 1987, as the dedication date for the building. It also listed Sir James Whitcombe's name, so I drew the conclusion that this had been one of his many contributions to the community.

I wondered how Miranda felt when she first came here and was made aware of all the ways that her birth father had been involved with the village of Carlton Heath. It saddened me that he had passed away before she could meet him. Someday I hoped to ask her about that time in her life.

"I should warn you," Miranda said. "Ellie makes it a practice to always dress in some sort of costume of her own for this special evening. She likes to keep it a surprise. It's not anything related to Dickens's era. She just comes up with her own clever creations. The first year I met her she was a sugar plum fairy. I think I still have pink glitter on my coat from when she hugged me that night."

I remembered how Ellie had been the most colorfully dressed woman at Ian and Miranda's wedding. At the time I thought it was because she liked wide-brimmed hats with audacious poppies and sunflowers. I never guessed how much she adored dressing up every day in her own style of happiness.

Tonight, when she opened the doors and let us inside the theater, she was wearing a beanie that had a whimsical star attached to the top. Around her neck and waist and hips were long strands of tiny Christmas lights that lit up and flashed on and off at different moments. The rest of her costume was green. All green. Even her hair was green. Pinned all over her in no particular order were ornaments. Lots of ornaments. I now understood why she wanted to buy so many tiny ornaments at Harrods the other day.

"O, Christmas tree, O, Christmas tree!" Ian sang as if recognizing her costume and singing about it was the secret password that opened the door.

"Yes, yes! Come in, come in." Ellie motioned for us to close the door behind us. To her dismay, guests were already coming up the walkway behind us. "We've an hour and a half till showtime. I don't know why people are arriving now."

One of the women in the group tapped on the door. She was wearing a costume that looked like what a Christmas caroler would wear during Dickens's time. Ian explained that we weren't ready to open the doors for at least another hour.

"We're here to help," the woman said. "We're the Rochester Carolers. We've come to sing."

"I didn't know we were expecting singers," Ellie said.

"Andrew MacGregor gave us a call this week. We're to sing as the guests arrive."

"Oh, yes!" The star attached to the top of Ellie's cap bobbed as she nodded. "The singers! Andrew told me. I'd completely forgotten."

"Where would you like us? Inside or out?"

"If you don't mind the chill, I think outside would be best. It's a mild evening, isn't it? But do stay inside and keep yourselves warm at least the next half an hour or so."

Ellie scurried off, her ornaments shimmering and her lights twinkling. "Edward?" She called out for him. "Edward? Can you see to the thermostat? I don't think it was turned on when we were here earlier today."

The bustling began and Miranda and I went to work, side by side, as we had the other night at the Tea Cosy. The theater had a convenient kitchen area with a refrigerator. Both the refrigerator and all the counter space were taken up with treats for the refreshment table.

We readied the beverages, decorated the refreshment table, and spread all the treats out in a festive manner with red cocktail napkins sprinkled throughout.

Julia came up behind us and let out a squeak. Miranda and I turned to see her in a darling mouse costume. She had news about the actors backstage. One of them had torn her costume and Ellie was doing a last-minute stitch up.

"Mrs. Roberts told me she was afraid she might forget her lines, so I practiced them with her." Julia beamed. "She only has two lines. But I know how stressful it can be when you're about to go onstage. Well, bye!"

"You definitely are part of a theatrical family," I said to Miranda.

"Yes. I am."

"Do you like to act?"

"No. Not at all. I know a lot of lines from a lot of plays, though. More Shakespeare than anything. I used to run around backstage the way Julia is. Never in a mouse costume, though."

We finished laying out the tea service on the table, using all the teaspoons available in the kitchen. The harmonizing carolers echoed in the foyer as they warmed up their voices before heading outside to add a merry welcoming touch for the arrival of the first guests.

The doors opened.

Ushers were in their places and Julia, the most convivial mouse that ever scampered around in a theater, was in high spirits. She received endless pats on the head as she expertly wove her way through the throng of people of all ages. I'd never been to the opening night of a play, so I didn't know if there was always this much merriment or if this was a British distinction. Or maybe it was characteristic of only this play, performed only on this night, with only this community.

Whatever the factors were, it made for a delightful time before the play even began. Ellie came to us with programs in her hand. "Miranda, why don't you and Anna find your seats and save a place for Ian? Go down the left side. Markie will show you where we've saved your places."

Tall Mark, wearing an impressive-looking suit for such a young man, proudly ushered us to the fourth row from the front. Ian was already seated. Miranda slid in next to him and I took the aisle seat.

The inside of the theater was as lush as the outside. The curtain was made of a deep blue–colored velvet and when it was drawn back by invisible cords, the lights dimmed and an impressive hush fell over the audience.

On center stage was my uncle Andrew, dressed in the most magnificent Father Christmas costume I'd ever seen. It was, as Miranda had said, very much like the one on the antique postcard hanging on the wall in her bathroom. I glanced over at Ian and saw the look of a son's great pride as he focused on his dad.

The spotlight warmed on Uncle Andrew's impressive figure. He turned to the audience and with the great rolling of the r's with his Scottish accent he quoted the first line of Dickens's *A Christmas Carol.*

"Marley was dead. As dead as a doornail."

Chapter Seventeen

I settled back in my plush seat and watched as the thoroughly enjoyable, impressive, and heartwarming play unfurled through the interpretation of the senior citizen actors. Each of them seemed to take their role quite seriously and played every scene with dramatic flair.

Petite Julia the mouse had joined us and was taking turns standing and sitting on Miranda's lap and then on my lap. She clapped softly with simple joy when she heard the line, "For it is good to be children sometimes, and never better than at Christmas, when its mighty Founder was a child himself."

At one point Miranda turned to me and whispered, "My mother would have loved this. I think of her every year when I see the play."

I gave her arm a squeeze.

In that moment, I felt as if I was a world away from my mother and father and the rest of my Minnesota relatives. While I didn't miss them necessarily, I did feel a fondness when I thought of them. I didn't think that my mother or any of my relatives would "love" the play as Miranda said her mother would have. They would enjoy it, no doubt. But the theater fell into the category of all things fanciful and frivolous.

As did my love of art and drawing.

Miranda tapped my arm and whispered. "That's our cue. We need to slide out before intermission and help at the refreshment table."

We left Julia with Ian and took our places behind the bountiful spread.

The guests of all ages were fun to watch and chat with. I especially enjoyed the enthusiastic comments from the younger theatergoers who proudly wanted me to know which one of the actors was their grandmother or great uncle.

I thought of Peter the most during intermission and wondered which one of the older couples was his parents. Some wistful part of me kept hoping he'd been able to slip away and would come striding up to the table at any moment and catch me by surprise.

But that didn't happen.

On this night, the Christmas wishes that were coming true were those wished by the cast. This was their night in the spotlight and they were giving such commendable performances. The most notable was the man who was playing the role of Scrooge. He was leading all of us to believe that he truly was being transformed that night.

When we returned to our seats, the curtains were drawn for the third and final act. Scrooge, still in his nightgown and nightcap, stepped onto the stage and the lights shone on a large, festively decorated Christmas tree. Mounds of wrapped gifts surrounded the tree and in the midst of it all was the imposing figure of my uncle in his Father Christmas costume.

"Come in, come in, and know me better, man." I loved the way Uncle Andrew belted out the line in his most jovial voice.

I glanced at Miranda and she was crying.

None of the scenes in the play affected me the same way as that one moment affected Miranda. That is, until Scrooge was being whisked away by the Spirit of Christmas Future. Julia was on my lap and her mouse tail was draped over the armrest and hanging in the aisle. Scrooge was shown the tiny crutches beside an empty stool by the fire and concluded that Tiny Tim had departed this earth.

Scrooge clutched his chest and cried out to the Spirit of Christmas Future, "I am not the man I was! Assure me that I may yet change these shadows you have shown me by an altered life."

I wasn't sure why that got to me but it did. I teared up and wished that Peter were beside me. Instead, I had Julia balanced on my lap, so I reached for one of the ears and blotted my tears.

Scrooge played out his transformation fabulously and delivered his well-known declaration, "I will honor Christmas in my heart, and try to keep it all the year." I felt a lump in my throat and lowered Julia on her feet so that we could stand together the moment the curtains began to close and be among the first to offer our wild applause.

"We need to get back to the table," Miranda whispered.

Reluctantly, this time, I slid out the back of the darkened

theater. The applause broke out just as we entered the brightly lit lobby.

"Just a minute," I told Miranda. I rushed back in and stood at the back, offering my applause. It seemed the right thing to do as the stage filled with the endearing cast. They received the hearty affirmation with many bows and grins and bobbing heads. I thought there might be some shenanigans with waves and kisses blown out to friends and family members. Not so. To the last, each of them maintained their role with dignity and reserved pride.

I hurried back to help Miranda tidy up. The packed playhouse let out a few minutes later and the slow stream of pleased guests made their way out the door where the Rochester Carolers were giving it their all once again. Some of the guests stopped by the refreshment table for one last tartlet or a bite of fudge. Most of the food had been enjoyed during the intermission. During the third act Ellie had consolidated what was left down to four small platters.

"We estimated quite well on the food this year," Ellie commented. She stood beside me behind the refreshment table. "I had my doubts earlier this week. But as usual, it all shifted out nicely."

An older couple wearing coats and matching red scarfs came over to the table. The man reached for a coconut macaroon, examining it before taking a bite.

"Oh! Hallo!" Ellie said. "How's Molly doing? I heard she's home with a fever. I hope that won't change your plans to come for Christmas."

I perked up, catching on that these were Peter's parents. I smiled politely, hoping to be introduced.

"We'll see how she does and ring you tomorrow. Would that be all right?" Peter's mother had a soft expression but a surprisingly wrinkled and weary-looking face. She gave the impression of being a very private person who had more than a few significant ailments of her own but none that she would ever complain about to others.

"Yes, give me a call once you know. We are all looking forward to having you join us."

Peter's father wore glasses and a hearing aid. His white hair was yellowed on the ends and looked scruffy, as if he was overdue for a haircut.

"Have you met Anna?" Ellie asked enthusiastically. "This is Andrew's niece. She's staying with us. She and her mother came from America last May for Ian and Miranda's wedding."

Peter's mother glanced at me and gave a polite nod. "We understand you are an artist."

"Yes." I wasn't used to being called that, but yes seemed to be the correct answer.

"Peter said you are making sketches of Whitcombe Manor."

I nodded again.

"How lovely."

I couldn't tell if she was trying to size me up or if she was simply being reserved and formal in her approach. The good thing was that at least Peter had said something to her about me. I had no way of knowing how much he'd said or how he'd framed the comments. But at least I was mentioned in his conversations with his family.

"If Molly is well, I suppose we will see you on Christmas, then." Peter's mother seemed to still be observing me carefully.

"Yes," I said with a sincere nod. "I hope she feels better soon."

Peter's parents gave me a polite farewell and made their exit.

"I must fly," Ellie said. "Are you and Miranda okay with cleaning everything up here?"

"Yes. We'll take care of it."

"I'm off to set up for the cast party, then."

I'd forgotten that Ellie was hosting the cast party at Whitcombe Manor. I'd spent the day leisurely at Miranda's while she must have been going a mile a minute getting everything ready.

"I'll help out at the cast party, too, Ellie. As soon as we're done here I'll be ready for you to put me to work at your place."

"Katharine has been at it, helping me all afternoon. She's already there, so take your time. This is really the easiest gathering every year. I just love it." Ellie started to bustle her swaying ornaments out the door but forgot something and turned around.

"Oh, dear! I nearly forgot. Julia asked if she could stay here and get a ride home with you. Whatever you do, please, don't leave here without my little mouse. Ian has the key. He said he'd lock up. Be sure to get everything turned off. Ian knows everything else that needs to be done. All right. I'm leaving now. Ta!"

A handful of guests lingered. Peter's parents were gone. I guessed that anyone who was connected to anyone who had anything to do with the play was already on their way to Whitcombe Manor. It didn't take long for Miranda and me to wrap the leftovers to take to the cast party.

We were ready to leave when we discovered one problem. Ian's sports car could only hold two people. They could slide Julia into the open wedge behind the two bucket seats and she liked that idea very much because she knew that her brother had ridden there before.

"I'll make two trips." Ian handed the key to the front entrance to Miranda. "Julia, why don't you stay here with Miranda? I'll take Anna over first and be back in a wink."

Just then the jolly man himself appeared, still wearing his Father Christmas costume. He pulled up in a compact car, not on a sleigh. But his arrival was most welcome.

Chapter Eighteen

*J*ulia begged to go with Ian and Miranda, so I gladly opted to go with Uncle Andrew. Once we were in the car my uncle said, "Are you able to confide in your old uncle?"

"Confide? About what?"

"Peter, of course. Has that young man expressed his honorable intentions toward you yet or do I need to put a lump of coal in his stocking this year?"

I smiled at my uncle. Inwardly, though, I was grimacing because I was getting tired of answering this question. "There are no honorable intentions to express."

"Are you telling me he's been dishonorable?"

"No, I'm telling you that there is nothing to report. Peter is a great guy. Very honorable. But there's nothing between us."

Uncle Andrew started the car and said in a jovial tone that matched his costume, "You didn't put him off, did you? On your big night on the town to see Ben. Ben with the handsome face and all the rest of it. You were clever with that one—I'll give you that. Clever enough. But when he showed you Londontown, tell me, daft girl, that you were nice to him."

"Of course I was nice to him. How did you know about Big Ben?"

Looking straight ahead at the road, he said, "I have ears. I have a window. When my window is open, I hear what's said from the garden below."

I tried to remember what Peter and I talked about on the back brick patio at the Tea Cosy. That had to be the conversation my uncle was referring to.

"Are you telling me you don't remember? God is the one holding the universe together; we are the ones who get out of sync. Fresh starts. Friends. And then the clever banter about the tall guy with the handsome face that lights up when he sees you."

"You really were doing a thorough job of eavesdropping, weren't you?"

Andrew glanced at me and asked, "Where do you think the term *eavesdropping* comes from? From those of us who live under the eaves and hear it all."

I let out a big sigh. We drove in silence for a short distance before he said, "I'm never wrong about these things. You know that I was the one who convinced Ian to meet Miranda. That turned out all right, didn't it?"

"Yes. It did."

"Well, then, I should be right about this match as well. It's a good match." Andrew glanced over at me and I returned a skeptical look.

"We shall see what we shall see," he said.

"Yes, we shall," I agreed.

Andrew steered the car through the opened gates and headed down the long drive to Whitcombe Manor. All the windows glowed with buttery warm light and even the windows on the second floor were lit up. The drive was lined with cars and we had to park some distance from the house. I took my uncle's arm as we walked. The gravel crunched beneath our feet and we could see our breath in the crisp night air.

There was something poetically enchanting about strolling arm in arm with Father Christmas under the towering trees on such a night, in such a place, headed to such a grand home filled with wonderful people. This moment was one that would long stay in my memory.

Andrew placed his hand on top of mine. "You don't mind me giving you a hard time, do you, lass?"

"No."

"You're sure, then?"

"It makes me feel like I'm family here. I like that. Very much."

"So do we, Anna. So do we."

I realized that everyone has their own set of peculiarities. If Andrew were my father, I'd undoubtedly find nothing charming about his interrogation and eavesdropping. The quirks that made Andrew endearing to me during this short visit would drive me crazy if I had to endure them all the time.

The same premise had to apply to my parents. They were good people. Kind, generous, and faithful. I'd grown too familiar with their way of showing interest and concern for my life.

That's why I couldn't wait to break out of the cocoon and test my wings.

I spotted the GRACE AND PEACE RESIDE HERE sign and thought of how those were the two qualities I wanted to be continually present and evident in my life.

Andrew and I entered the manor and were swept into a wave of festive guests laughing, singing, dancing, and raising their glasses in a toast to the Whitcombes. The many costumed senior citizens made it feel as if we'd stepped into a timeless version of the sketch of Fezziwig's Ball Ellie had selected for the programs. All that was missing was the fiddler.

When the guests saw Father Christmas had arrived, another cheer rose and another round of toasts. My uncle played the part, moving among the guests with a mild demeanor, asking what gift they'd like Father Christmas to bring them that year and then tilting his head back and filling the air with his roaring laughter.

I slid through the thickest part of the guests and headed for the kitchen to see if Ellie needed any help. She was filling the teakettle with water when I entered. "Oh, good! You've come. Can you help me see to the drinks? We have far more people than ever before. I wasn't expecting so many. We need tea and coffee and more cans of soft drinks added to the table in the drawing room."

"I'd be glad to do that." I took the kettle from her and plugged it in while she began stacking cans of soft drinks onto a tray.

"They've all decided to congregate in the entry. It's the strangest thing. And the dancing is new. We've never had dancing before. It's these pensioners. They need to get out more. They've all gone a bit wild."

I'd come to know my way around the kitchen well enough over the last few days. When Ellie headed out the door with the tray full of soft drinks, I went about making several pots of tea and brewing a fresh pot of coffee. I checked the refrigerator to see if all the food had been put out or if we had backup trays of "nibbles" as Ellie and Miranda had called them. The refrigerator was nearly empty except for a half a jar of olives and some leftover sandwiches from lunch.

I poured the olives into a bowl and took them with me as I delivered a pot of tea to the serving table in the drawing room. Surprisingly, there was still plenty of food on the trays. Nearly all the cakes and cookies were gone, though. The dancing seniors, it seemed, were more interested in caffeine and sugar than in the mini quiches, sausages, and ham sandwiches. They reminded me of teenage girls at a sleepover.

Once I had replenished the coffee and put out more cups and mugs, I stood back and watched the ever-changing kaleidoscope of color and movement and cheery laughter that filled the manor. It was a house made for a night such as this.

My eyes roamed the entry hall, looking for Peter.

It was possible, wasn't it? That he had decided to come to the cast party after his parents returned home? Peter had been the main source of entertainment the other night at the Tea Cosy. That was only a night of soup and bread. What kind of fun and bedlam could he stir up at a party like this where the guests were already in high spirits?

I walked through the downstairs rooms looking for Peter. I wanted to see his face. I wanted to watch from across the room as he effortlessly gathered a circle of admirers and got them to laugh in a way that made them believe they were young again.

But Peter wasn't there.

As I watched the cast, I thought of my parents. How would they fit in if they were here? I remembered the way my mother had hung back at the wedding. She would probably not be dancing at this party, either.

I wondered what my parents were doing. If the next few days were going to be as full as the last few days had been, I decided that this might be a good time to call them.

Heading up the stairs, I turned on the light in the guest room and pulled out my phone. It took a few attempts before the connection went through. On the fourth ring my father answered.

"Hi, Dad."

"Anna? Is everything all right? Are you okay?"

"I'm fine. Everything is great. I'm having a really nice time."

"Why did you call, then?"

"I just wanted to say hi to you and Mom."

He didn't reply.

"And I wanted to tell you both that I love you."

"That's nice of you, Anna. Very nice. Here's your mother. Say hello to her."

"Anna?"

"Hi, Mom."

"What's wrong?"

I grinned and leaned my head back. "Nothing is wrong. Everything is very good. I'm having a wonderful time."

"Did you call just to tell us that?"

"Yes. I also called to tell you that I love you and I hope you and Dad have a really nice Christmas. Give Opa a kiss for me."

"Are you sure you're okay?"

"Yes. I'm very sure. How is everything there? Has it been snowing?"

"We had a little snow yesterday. Not much. Everything is quiet here. We're all fine."

"That's good."

"You're still planning to come home on Tuesday, aren't you? You haven't decided to stay there longer this time?"

"No. I'm still planning to come home on Tuesday. But Edward and Ellie invited me to come back. They offered to pay my way because they want to hire me to do some sketches for them of Whitcombe Manor."

"When would you go back?"

"Ellie suggested I come in the spring. She said I could stay as long as I wanted."

There was silence on the other end.

"Mom?"

"This is something that you want very much, isn't it?" My mother's tone was serious but I thought I heard softness in her words.

"Yes. I'd like to come back."

"What about Peter? Have you seen him?"

"Yes. I've seen him a few times."

Another pause followed.

"Be careful, Anna. That's all I would say to you. Be careful and guard your heart."

"I will, Mom. I promise. I will."

"Merry Christmas, Anna."

"Merry Christmas, Mom."

All in all, I thought the small gift of words she had just given me made a fine gift. She acknowledged that being here was important to me. I was grateful. And I was being careful.

Chapter Nineteen

 $\mathcal{I}$ went back downstairs only to discover that the cast party had come to an abrupt conclusion.

While I was on the phone upstairs, one of the women had thrown out her hip and was being taken away in a stretcher. She waved and was smiling and telling the others this happened before and it was nothing a little rest after a good chiropractic adjustment wouldn't fix.

The other partiers looked around at each other, unconvinced that hers would be a speedy recovery. They seemed to sober up as if she represented the Spirit of Christmas to Come if they continued as if they were at Fezziwig's Ball.

One by one I watched them go for their coats and scarves and make a short speech expressing their appreciation to Edward and Ellie, who stood at the door. I started picking up cups and plates that had been abandoned on the stairs.

"Well!" Ellie exclaimed when the house was back to its emptied, echoey self. "That was unusual."

Edward, Ellie's reserved and careful husband, looked down at his wife, who was still dressed as a Christmas tree with her star-topper cap tilted to the side.

With a wry expression he said, "Yes. Quite unusual." It was clear that he meant that his wife was the real quite unusual attraction at Whitcombe Manor that evening. But he wouldn't have it any other way.

Ellie clapped her hands together and one of the ornaments affixed near her elbow fell off. "Good news for all us weary souls. I have hired a crew to come in tomorrow morning and put everything aright, so for us, it's off to bed and no cleaning up tonight."

Edward, Mark, and I were the only ones left in the great hall. I didn't know if other lingering guests and friends had found their way into the kitchen, living room, or study. But I, for one, was very glad to take Ellie up on her directive to go to bed.

I took a warm bath and wrapped my hair up into a cinnamon roll–style bun on the top of my head. When I got into bed that night, I was ready to sleep but more importantly, I wanted to dream.

I don't know how long I slept or if I dreamed at all. I awoke, as I had on my first morning at Whitcombe Manor, squinting to see the light of the new day edging its way in between the drapes. It wasn't the light that stirred me from my slumber. This morning I woke because I thought I heard something at the window.

Pulling the comforter up to my chin, I listened carefully. Was it hail? A woodpecker? Or was it the Spirit of Christmas Past, Present, or Future here to take me on a life-altering journey?

Carefully padding over to the window, I pulled the drapes

back far enough to look down on the wintering gardens. A ready smile came, causing my lips as well as my spirits to rise like the dawn.

Peter was standing in the center of the garden.

He had a fistful of pebbles and was tossing them at my guest room window. I waved and wondered if he realized that he was standing where we'd stood together when we danced last May. As a matter of fact, he was just about in the spot where we had shared the unintended kiss that had launched the unraveling of my cocoon.

I tried to figure out how to open the guest room window but it appeared to be permanently sealed on all sides. I waved and held up my open palm, indicating that he should wait there.

Peter pointed to his bicycle that was parked to the side by a large tree. It was the bike with the wagon seat in the front. I realized what was happening. He was inviting me to go with him on his morning bike ride that he'd told me about the other night in the taxi.

I scurried around, pulling on a pair of jeans, rummaging for a clean top, and pulling a warm fisherman cable-knit sweater over my head. I undid my sleep-frazzled hair and gave it a shake.

Julia's prince comment from the morning on the lawn came back to me. I wasn't exactly in the turret portion of this grand castle and the prince wasn't climbing up my hair. But he had come to me, Romeo style, and we were going to go for a "gorgeous ride" as he'd called it.

Grabbing a scarf, I took the stairs as quietly as I could. I pulled on my socks and boots and opened the front door.

Peter was standing in the alcove. His bike was waiting behind him. He grinned but didn't say anything. I stood there, breathless, with nothing clever coming to mind.

He held out his hand to me and said, "Nice morning for a gorgeous ride, don't you think?"

I slipped my hand in his and wondered for a moment if I was still asleep and if this was the dream I'd hoped would come to me in the night. The roughness of his hand and the cool sensation of his palm clasping mine made it evident that I was awake. Wide awake and ready to ride off from the castle.

Peter steadied the bike as I got into the wagon. It was a tight squeeze but comfy enough. I settled in and he got on the seat.

"Hold on."

I grasped the sides of the wagon and off we went, bumping our way down the gravel driveway. I laughed out loud.

"What's so funny?" he asked.

"It tickles!" I'm sure I must have looked ridiculous, a grown woman folded up in a child's wagon seat like that. Saying that it tickled must have sounded ridiculous, too. I didn't care. I loved that he had schemed up this little rendezvous.

"How's your sister?" I called over my shoulder.

"Molly is much better. Thank you for asking. How was the play?"

"Great! It was well done and a lot of fun."

"That's what my parents said."

"Did they tell you we met?"

"Yes. How did that go?"

"It was a short conversation."

"My parents are reserved."

"So are mine. I called them last night just to say hi. They kept asking if something was wrong."

"What did you tell them?"

"I told them I was fine and everything was going great. Then I said I hoped to return in the spring."

"So you're serious about returning, then?"

"Yes. I want to finish the sketches of Whitcombe Manor. I haven't gotten very far."

"I suppose you'd get a lot further along if people didn't keep taking you around London or kidnapping you at all hours and gallivanting around the countryside."

I laughed. "Is that what we're doing? Gallivanting?"

"Yes. Gallivanting. I don't even know if that's a word people use anymore or if that's the right way to use it. But let's pretend it is. Now tell me, how are you enjoying the gallivanting so far?"

I leaned back in the wagon like a lady of leisure with my hands still holding tightly to either side. "It's wonderful. You can enjoy the view and have your backside massaged at the same time."

Peter said, "Since you enjoy the outdoors, you should plan to go glamping when you come back in the spring."

"Now you really are making up words."

"No. I'm not. Glamping is a real word. It's camping but they put you up in large heated tents on raised wooden floors. The tents are big yurts. You know, they go up in the center. It's popular in the area where Beatrix Potter's home is located. You have the luxury of a comfortable place to sleep and civilized food to eat."

"It sounds like a British-style safari from the last century, like in the movies."

"Exactly. Teatime at four every day. The biggest difference would be that in Africa you'd have elephants and lions roaming about. At Windermere Lake you'd only have sheep. And an occasional fox, I suppose."

Peter was pedaling down the country lane now. The morning mist was rising and in the tranquility I could hear the chittering of birds in the distance.

"What do you think?" he asked.

"Glamping sounds like fun. I'd like to try it."

"It's a nice morning, isn't it?"

"It's gorgeous. Just like you said." We rode on and I was so happy and content that I started humming.

"Would you like some coffee?" Peter asked.

"Sure."

I'd been down this same road a half dozen times and was pretty sure there weren't any cafés or other places to get coffee in this direction. We'd have to be going the opposite direction and heading into town to the Tea Cosy if we were going to get something to drink.

But if "gallivanting" was what we were doing and *glamping* was a real word, then maybe there was a woodland café run by fairies a little farther down the trail.

After all, he was the driver and I was just along for the ride.

And what a gorgeous ride it was.

Chapter Twenty

*P*eter soon led us off the main road onto a well-worn trail. He maneuvered through a muddy patch of the trail and through a glen. When we came out on the other side, I knew where we were. We were on our way to Rose Cottage.

He continued pedaling down a very bumpy path and turned toward the cottage. We stopped by the rock wall and after he helped me get out of the wagon, we took the stone steps up the walkway to the front door. "It's still pretty early," I said. "Are you sure it's going to be all right if we disturb them?"

"Let's see if they're up." Peter pounded on the doorframe with his open palm.

When Ian opened the door, fully dressed and with a grin, I knew this was all planned.

"We need some coffee," Peter said. "Do you know where we might find some?"

"I think we have some for you wayfarers." Ian stood back and held the door open. "Miranda, we have some vagrants that have come calling. Can we spare them a bit of Christmas cheer?"

The scrumptious fragrance of dark coffee and muffins baking in the oven filled our nostrils. Ian leaned over and kissed me on the cheek as I entered. Miranda received an effortless greeting kiss from Peter and then gave me a tender hug and kiss on the cheek. I was beginning to fall into the local way of giving and receiving airy greeting kisses.

"Were you surprised?" Miranda asked.

"Yes." I leaned closer and whispered, "I thought I was in a dream."

"Good. I hope you keep feeling that way."

I turned to look at Peter. He appeared quite proud of himself for pulling off the surprise.

"What time did you guys have to get up to do all this?" I pulled my heavy sweater over my head, hung it on the coat hook with my scarf, and left my boots by the door.

"Not very early," Ian said. "Come on. Sit by the fire. The coffee is ready. Miranda said she knows the way you like it: nice and dark."

What followed was the merriest, most spontaneous Christmas Eve morning breakfast I could ever have imagined. We talked and laughed and did what close friends do during the holidays. I'd never experienced anything like this before and I wanted to cry. The tears I kept blinking back were because of the loveliness of it all and also because I knew that when I went home in a few days, I wouldn't have anything like this.

Ian started telling a story about how he had pulled off a

surprise on Peter's birthday a few years ago. "Everyone at the office came in early by fifteen minutes. When Peter arrived, it looked as if all of us had been there since dawn working on an important project. He came strolling in and thought he'd missed the notice about the early arrival."

Peter shook his head as if the memory was slightly painful. At the least, it had embarrassed him. That was a look I was all too familiar with but not one he seemed to wear often.

"We all put on that we were frantic for coffee. Peter agreed to go around and get everyone's order and dash out to get it for us. He had no choice. We shamed him into doing it."

"You were brutal," Peter said. "I don't know where you all came up with such nonsensical orders. Half-caff, nonfat, soy latte with an extra shot and extra hot." He shook his head again.

"Oh, so you remember my order after all," Ian teased.

"Did you remember everyone's order?" I asked.

"I wrote them down. And everyone kept correcting me and saying I'd written the wrong thing or that they'd changed their minds. It was pandemonium over morning coffee. You wouldn't have believed it."

"When did you catch on that they were giving you a hard time?"

Peter looked at Ian and gave him a smirk. "Not until I got to the front of the line at the crowded coffee shop with my list. I looked up and there was Ian behind the counter, wearing a green apron and putting on an act as if he worked there. Everyone at the coffee shop was in on it. They had a cake waiting for me."

"And coffees, too, I hope."

"For everyone else, yes. For me, I've avoided coffee ever since that day." He gave Miranda a chin-up look and lifted his Christmas mug that had already been refilled twice with Miranda's special blend. "That is, until today."

"All I know," Miranda said, "is that whatever prank my husband pulled on you, you deserved it after what you did to me the first time we had you here for supper."

"What did I do?" Peter looked so innocent. His short brown hair was still scruffy from the bike ride. His soft blue eyes looked bright in the glow of the Christmas tree lights and undoubtedly due to the fact that he'd had three cups of coffee.

"I served pasta." Miranda waited with her dark eyebrows raised as if waiting for him to remember and add his part to the tale.

"Oh, right. With the shrimp and garlic and capers."

"Yes. With the shrimp and garlic and capers. And lots of Parmesan on top." Miranda turned to me. "I put the plate in front of him and he just stared at it."

"I was taking a moment to offer up a prayer of gratefulness."

Now it was Miranda's turn to shake her head as the story was unfolding. "I thought maybe he had food allergies and was trying to decipher all the ingredients. I asked if he was okay with what I'd made."

Peter grinned at the memory. "I told her I did have a few allergies, actually."

"First he said he had an allergy to shellfish. And garlic. What were the rest?"

"I told her I was lactose intolerant, could only eat gluten-free pasta, and that capers tend to put me into anaphylactic shock. But other than that, her meal looked just fine."

"You didn't believe him, did you?" I asked.

"For about two seconds."

I looked at Peter and said, "All this makes me wonder. Why should I believe that glamping is a real thing?"

"It is," Ian said in Peter's defense. "I've been glamping. It's great fun. Miranda hasn't gone yet. Maybe we should plan a trip for next summer."

Miranda cleared her throat.

Ian quickly corrected himself. "Why wait for summer? We could try for early spring. When are you coming back, Anna?"

"I don't know yet."

"You've got to be here for my dad's birthday in July." Ian told about the birthday gathering last summer when he got ahold of one of the helium balloons and went around startling all the older women by speaking to them in a squeaky, helium-altered voice.

"One of these days you will have to join the rest of us who act our age." Peter said it in a good-natured way but his comment caused Ian to pause and take on a more serious expression.

Ian looked at Miranda. She smiled, mostly with her eyes. Her head bobbed slightly.

Rising to his feet and standing by the fire with his arm resting on the mantel, Ian said, "You're right, my friend. And it seems that day has come."

I watched my cousin carefully, not sure if he was about to give a meaningful speech by the hearth or if this was one of his jokes.

"Miranda and I..." Ian paused. "Well, in truth, it's going to be all Miranda from this point on. But you see..." He looked over at his wife.

Miranda's face was pink and her lips were pressed together as she gazed back at him with deep affection.

I knew what Ian was about to say next. My hand rose to cover my mouth so that I wouldn't blurt out the glad news for them.

Ian's voice rose with pride. "We're going to have a baby."

Chapter Twenty-One

*O*nce the cheers and hugs and handshakes were all undertaken with much joy, Ian returned to his place next to Miranda on the love seat. He took her hand and Miranda said, "Please don't say anything to anyone. We really wanted to make the big announcement at Christmas dinner so that we tell everyone on both sides of the family at the same time."

"We're the first ones you've told?" I asked.

"Yes." Miranda glanced at Ian. "And there's a reason for that."

"We've talked about it," Ian said, "and we have both agreed that we'd like the two of you to stand in as our child's godparents."

I felt a sweet rush of excitement at Ian's request. My family didn't have a tradition of appointing godparents, so I wasn't sure what it entailed, but I was honored to be invited and to be included as a special part of their family this way.

"I'd love to," I said quickly. "Yes, of course. What an honor."

The three of us turned to Peter. His expression had clouded and he looked as if he was still seriously weighing the pros and cons of such a responsibility. That's when I realized I may have spoken too swiftly. I didn't know what that tradition meant here in England. I had assumed it meant that I would be actively interested and involved in their child's life, which appealed to me very much.

In a somber tone Peter said, "If anything happens to the two of you, it would fall to Anna and me to raise your child."

Ian nodded. He looked serious, but not too serious. In the starburst of such happy news, leaving his child as an orphan was the last thing Ian seemed to be considering.

Peter, however, seemed to be taking his time as he considered that possibility. His hesitation cast a solemn cloud over what had been a joyous gathering.

Is Peter hesitating because Ian and Miranda said they wanted to name me as the counterpart? What is it that I'm not understanding here about the role of godparents?

"I'd like to give it some thought," Peter said.

"Fair enough," Ian replied. "Take your time. You've got until the end of July."

"Or possibly the first week of August." Miranda turned to me. "I almost said something earlier when you were talking about returning in the spring and when Ian suggested we all go glamping. I wondered if you would consider coming in late summer instead and staying through the fall?"

"Or come both times," Ian said. "Better yet, why don't you move here? We'd all be in favor of that, wouldn't we?"

Ian looked over at Peter. He seemed to still be lost in thought over the complexities of being a godfather.

"Is there something I should know?" I asked.

Peter's chin lifted with a quick snap. He looked at me with raised eyebrows.

"About being a godparent, I mean. Is there more to what I just agreed to than I know?" I released a nervous chuckle, hoping it might help alleviate the somberness that had filled the room. "If there is something I'm missing about this, please tell me now."

"It's no small commitment to raise a child," Peter said with his stoic expression remaining.

We all knew how much Peter had taken on by helping to raise his sister. No one wanted to diminish that factor in his life. Perhaps the thought of being committed to two children was more than he was willing to process. I thought about what Ian had said the day before about how Peter needed to move ahead with his own life apart from the needs of Molly.

"Don't take me wrong," Peter said. "I couldn't be happier for the two of you. I need to think through my part, though."

The way that Peter was taking this so seriously made me agree for the first time that maybe Ian was right. Peter did have too much loyalty for his own good.

Fortunately, Ian managed to turn the tense moment into a lighter one by suggesting that we join in a toast to the new little one. He went to the kitchen and pulled out four fluted glasses. In the refrigerator he had a bottle of sparkling pear juice that he and Miranda had chilled and saved for this moment.

We clinked our glasses, offered another round of cheering

congratulations, and to my relief, Peter's countenance returned to one of happiness for Ian and Miranda. Our breakfast time wound down and Peter said he needed to get going.

Instead of riding back with Peter, I opted to stay at Ian and Miranda's. I'd left my sketching supplies there when we went to the play last night. I explained to Peter that I had a Christmas gift I was still working on.

Miranda nudged me as if trying to get me to give Peter the gift for Molly before he left. It was there, by the door, in my shoulder bag. The timing didn't feel right to me, though. Peter appeared to still be in deep contemplation and a children's book might add more anxiety to him right now. Besides, the book wasn't wrapped and if I was going to give it as a gift, I wanted it to look like one.

Peter gave me a casual good-bye kiss. This time my calculations had improved and as soon as he started to lean toward me, I turned my head just enough. His feathery gesture landed between my ear and my cheek and not in my hair like last time. I felt a sense of cultural accomplishment. I knew how to blend in with the hellos and good-byes without constantly giving away the fact that I was an American.

"Thanks for the gorgeous ride," I called out from the open door of the cottage.

Peter turned and waved. I couldn't help but think that he still looked sad. Or maybe it was his way of being serious. I remembered the way he'd furrowed his eyebrows when he went through the list of facts about Big Ben. Ten feet of concrete. Cast iron. Limestone something or other.

Maybe this is how he processes life. He needs measurements and a thorough understanding of the materials. He wants to know if there are potential flaws.

I grabbed a dish towel and helped Ian dry the dishes. I remembered how Peter knew exactly how much the clock tower had shifted over the years and how it had tilted so many millimeters to the north. *Or was it to the east?*

"Ian? Do you know that Big Ben is shifting?"

He gave me the most peculiar look.

"Big Ben. The clock tower at Parliament. It's shifting on its foundation."

"Yes."

"You knew that."

"Yes."

"Is that an architectural thing? Facts and planning and measuring?"

Ian chuckled. "I don't suppose we'd be very successful as architects if we didn't check the facts and do extensive planning and measuring."

"I think that's what Peter is doing," I said. "About the invitation to be a godparent. He seemed so serious about it like he was measuring and calculating what could go wrong. I just wondered if that's how he is."

Miranda and Ian exchanged glances.

"That's a great insight," Miranda said. "He definitely has a serious side to him. More serious than this guy." She gave Ian a playful tap with her elbow.

Ian took the dish towel and gave Miranda an equally playful snap with the end of it. "I'd stick around here and defend the

depth of my seriousness as well as my knowledge of which buildings in London are sliding into the Thames, but I have to leave
you two. My dad is making the rounds at the hospital this afternoon in his Father Christmas robe and I'm his understudy."

"Remember! Don't say anything to your dad yet." Miranda patted her midriff.

"You can count on me." Ian planted a kiss on her lips and gave
her a big hug. "I'll be back in plenty of time for the Christmas Eve
service tonight."

Miranda and I settled into the same easy pace we'd shared
the day before at Rose Cottage. I finished sketching the princess
scenes in the coloring book for Julia and wrapped the book for
Molly. I'd brought a few small gifts with me from home and was
glad that I had a little something for Ian and Miranda as well as
Edward, Ellie, and Mark, as well as for Andrew and Katharine. I
tried to convince myself that the book for Peter and Molly would
be taken as nothing more than a kind gesture. Giving it to him
shouldn't feel awkward. It wasn't as if there was any reason why
he should have a gift to exchange with me. I told myself things
were as they should be.

Friends. Just good friends.

I'd be back in the spring. Or the summer. Or maybe I'd end up
moving here as Ian suggested. Clearly, the way Peter did things
was with meticulous consideration of all the facts. If we were in the
process of building something lasting, then maybe we were still in
the process of pouring the ten-foot-thick cement foundation.

I was okay with that. It was good to have people in my life
who were anchored in reality.

That didn't keep me from dreaming, though. How could I not give way to fairy-tale possibilities of a Christmas yet to be? Not after the way I'd been awoken this morning with pebbles on my windowpane and a planned surprise breakfast at the end of the gorgeous bike ride.

Chapter Twenty-Two

I returned to Whitcombe Manor in the late afternoon and managed to find just enough time to slip my simple gifts under the Christmas tree and then get freshened up and dressed. The whole manor had been professionally cleaned while I was gone and my guest bathroom was replenished with fresh towels and bars of soap. I felt spoiled.

Julia was delighted that I was riding to church with them for the Christmas Eve service and chattered all the way. She and her mom wore matching red velvet dresses. Ellie's hair had returned to a dark auburn color after the Christmas-tree green from the night before. Edward and Mark wore dark suits and maintained a solemn posture as we entered the chapel.

The door of the sandstone chapel was festooned with evergreen garlands. Dozens of glowing candles were affixed to the standing candelabras at the front. The sacred space had a completely different feel than it had when I was last seated on one of these old wooden pews for Ian and Miranda's wedding.

We slid into the pew behind Ian and Miranda, who were seated with Andrew and Katharine. I glanced around as more people entered and moved in close together on the pews. I didn't see Peter and his parents and Molly yet. I didn't remember Peter saying that he would see me at the church that evening. It had been part of the conversation at breakfast so I assumed he would be there.

I had no success in spotting him, so I turned forward and fixed my gaze on the stained glass window at the front of the chapel behind the altar. I remembered studying it during the wedding and thinking that the blond Christ figure that was portrayed skill- fully and beautifully in the stained glass was more of a King Arthur figure than the usual image of a dark-haired Christ. What I liked about the work of art was that it gave the impression that Jesus was the Beloved of the Father as well as the omnipotent ruler of all.

A slender woman wearing an elegant, long black dress rose from the front row and took her place at the front of the chapel. From down the center aisle the minister strode with slow steps toward the pulpit. He was reading from a large, open Bible in his hands as he walked.

"For unto you is born this day in the city of David a Savior, who is Christ the Lord. And this shall be a sign unto you. You will find the babe wrapped in swaddling clothes and lying in a manger."

I saw Ian slide his arm around Miranda's shoulders and give her a squeeze.

Next Christmas Eve, Lord willing, they will have their own babe wrapped up in their arms.

The minister finished the reading at the same moment that he reached the pulpit. Without accompaniment, the woman at the front began singing a dramatic, angelic-sounding version of "O Holy Night." I felt my heart flutter.

This song! I wish I could look at Peter right now. I wish he were sitting beside me. I'd slip my arm through his again. This Christmas carol will always make me think of Peter and London and this beautiful service. Such divine memories.

I smiled to myself at the choice of my description for the memories.

Yes, divine. Divine memories.

When the soloist got to the line in the carol, "A thrill of hope, the weary world rejoices, for yonder breaks a new and glorious morn," I wanted to fall on my knees. I wanted to believe in a new and glorious morn. I understood what Miranda had said about feeling close to God when she was in this chapel during her first Christmas in Carlton Heath.

I felt His presence here, too.

It seemed in that moment that the past and present came together for me in this holy place. The "thrill of hope" was becoming the thrill of trusting God fully with all that was yet to be. He had always been the Spirit of Christmas, past, present, and future. My times were in His hands.

The rest of the service was filled with reverent, meaningful reminders of grace and hope and truth and light. We concluded by lighting candles, passing the light down the aisle, each of us giving what we had to the person beside us. We stood as a con-gregation, holding our burning candles aloft and singing "Silent Night."

The air seemed to crackle with true Christmas cheer. Hope permeated the moment and brought a glow to every face, even after the flames were blown out and the candles deposited in bins at the end of each aisle.

I lingered in the pew. I wanted to soak in the final essence of holiness and joy that still floated in the air disguised as the scent of snuffed candlewicks. My heart was happy.

I turned to go and that's when I saw Peter. He came toward me. I eagerly moved to the center aisle toward him. I was eager to give and receive a "holy kiss" of greeting in this sweet and holy place. Now that I'd figured out the right angle for the tilt of my head, I wanted to try it out.

The chapel was nearly emptied of faithful worshippers when Peter and I met in the aisle. We were standing in the center of the chapel. I felt so much affection for him right then. I leaned in but for some reason, he did not. I pulled back, not sure what the protocol was in a church.

Do we not greet each other with a kiss here?

Peter's expression was as serious as it had been that morning at Ian and Miranda's. "I need to say something to you."

"Okay."

"You have this way about you." He looked nervous, which was always such a surprising expression to see on him because he usu-ally appeared so confident. "You make people hope."

"That's a good thing, isn't it?"

He scratched his forehead and looked uncomfortable. I touched his arm and said, "What is it? What's wrong?"

"It's Molly."

"Is she sick?"

"No, she's fine. It's just that this week, while you've been here, I've been acting as if I have a normal life. I've been giving space to my own Christmas wishes, as you call them."

"And what is wrong with that?"

"It's Molly, you see. Molly is my responsibility. She will be the rest of my life." He gave me a pained expression. "I want you to understand that if the circumstances were different, I would be pursuing you right now like a wild man."

"Like a wild man?" I felt my lips turn up in a half grin.

He tempered his expression. "Like a gentleman is what I should have said. Like a gentleman who is able to make good on his intentions. A man who keeps his promises."

"You certainly are a man who keeps his promises." I added Ian's observation and said, "If anything, you've got too much integrity."

Peter shook his head vigorously. "You don't know the whole story, Anna."

I waited for him to go on. But he didn't. He looked down, struggling to say what he'd intended.

"What is it, Peter? What do you want to say?"

He lifted his chin and met my gaze. "I can't be your friend, Anna. I just can't. I thought I could. I thought that when you left after the wedding, I'd be able to forget about you but I couldn't. When you came back, I thought I could be around you in a casual way as friends." He shook his head. "It's not working."

I felt my pulse throbbing in my neck and I tightened my jaw. Even though my experience in romantic relationships was miniscule, I knew enough to realize that the way Peter was setting things up, this conversation could go two different directions. One way would be the happiest answer to all my dreams. The other way could devastate me.

"The truth is, I care deeply for you, Anna. There is so much about you that is extraordinary. That night in London..." His eyes met mine. "That night was divine. That's the only word I can think of. And then this morning it struck me when Ian and Miranda asked us to be godparents that..."

I swallowed, still not sure which way this was going to go.

"I can't. I can't pretend." He reached over and took my hand in his. My heart leapt at the tenderness of his touch.

He quickly let go of my hand as if he hadn't meant to touch me. He looked heartsick.

"Anna, I would never want to put on you the heavy responsibilities that come with me, with my life. I could never ask that of you."

"What are you saying?"

"I'm saying it wouldn't be fair to ask you to become a part of my life."

I let Peter's antiproposal sink in. The logical side of me stepped to the forefront of my thoughts. It was the voice of Prudence. She was speaking truth and I was listening.

"So, you're saying that you'd like to be more than friends but you can't because of your responsibilities."

"Exactly."

"But now we can't even be friends because you think it would be unfair for me or for us to keep hoping for more."

"Yes. That's it. You've said it better than I." He waited for me to speak again, looking like a man waiting for a pardon.

"I don't agree." My bold words surprised me.

They surprised Peter even more. For a shy girl given to fairy tales, I still knew poor logic when I saw it.

"Peter, don't you think I should be the one who gets to decide what's fair? You get to ask the question, responsibilities included. I get to answer. That's fair. I get to choose. You've not even asked the question or given me a chance to answer. That's what feels unfair to me."

Peter was caught off guard by my logical declaration.

I wasn't finished. One more piece of truth needed to be spoken. I knew if I didn't let it fly out of my mouth now, it never would.

"I understand that Molly is an important person in your life. I honor that. But Peter, she doesn't have to be the only woman in your life that you care about. She's your sister. That's all."

He pulled back and I could tell I'd overstepped some sort of boundary.

Peter and I were the only ones left inside the chapel. The candles had all been extinguished. The only illumination around us came from the dull amber glow of the dimmed overhead lights. It was difficult to read body language and expressions. I couldn't see his eyes clearly but it appeared to me that he had teared up.

"Anna." His voice was a firm whisper. "I have to tell you something so that you will understand. I have never told this to anyone. Not to Ian, not to anyone in Carlton Heath. I need to trust that you will keep this between us."

"Of course." Everything inside me wanted to wrap my arms around him and hold him close. Instead, I stood where I was, not moving, barely blinking. I wanted him to be able to read in my eyes that he could trust me with whatever he needed to say.

"Anna, Molly is not my sister." He drew in a quick breath and whispered, "She's my daughter."

Chapter Twenty-Three

No words found their way to my lips for some time.

The plan for the rest of the evening, that we'd set up at breakfast that morning, was for me to join Andrew and Katharine and gather at Rose Cottage. When we all agreed to the small celebration, I pictured Peter being part of it. Now I wasn't sure what was going to happen.

As Peter drove me to Rose Cottage, a light rain fell. I invited him by my silence to say everything he wanted to say in the privacy of his closed-up car.

He told me his story. It was his whole story, he said. Filled with lots of details that he said he'd never shared with anyone.

We stopped beside the stone wall in front of Rose Cottage and sat in the car for another ten minutes. The fine raindrops fell silently on the windshield. Inwardly tears were falling silently in my heart. Peter sounded so resolved. So determined to shoulder the responsibility of his choices and his circumstances. The sadness was there, in the corner of his eyes, just as I'd first noticed when we danced at the wedding. That sadness marked him. It chained him.

"I think it's best if I don't come in." Peter released a heavy sigh. I hoped that by opening up to me he might be able to feel at least a bit of the weight being lifted off of him. He shouldn't have held all this in for so long. And he shouldn't think that his past was going to limit his future.

Mentally, I was preparing a rousing inspirational talk on how he needed to release all this. He needed to let the "thrill of hope" come to him and trust God in a new way. I thought of the line in the carol, "till He appeared and the soul felt its worth." I wanted him to feel that. And to believe, as I had in the chapel, that a new and glorious morn could break for him if only he would release the past, accept the present, and be open to receiving love in the future.

But those were all discoveries he would have to make on his own. I didn't say any of the passionate thoughts that were bubbling inside me. I'd seen how concentrated and intense he could be when he was evaluating a decision. It didn't seem likely that I could convince him of anything right now. He was an architect. He knew that an existing structure had to be torn down or at least restructured before anything new and lasting could be built on the same foundation.

He leaned back, lifting his chin, indicating that we'd come to the end of our conversation. "I appreciate you listening and understanding why I've come to this conclusion."

I nodded. Then I knew I had to say something. "Peter, I

appreciate you entrusting me with your story. I'm not sure I understand the conclusions you've reached. But I respect them because they're your decisions."

As soon as I started to speak, my emotions rose to the surface. I wasn't sitting back, listening and trying to be understanding. I was now engaged in the conversation and no longer felt objective. I felt as I had in the chapel, that he was being unfair by unilaterally making a decision for both of us.

I opened my own door to get out but froze. It was as if all my sweet patience, understanding, and philosophical imagery had gotten out of the car and left me alone with my bruised little heart, sitting next to Peter. I couldn't look at him. I was mad. So mad.

"Peter? Would you consider one thing?" I turned to look at him even though I knew that tears were gathering in the corner of my eyes.

He looked at me with a guarded nod in the dim light.

"Would you just consider what your life might be like if you gave yourself some grace?"

I wasn't sure if my words had settled on him. I kept going, careful to not pour out everything I was thinking and feeling.

"I understand the high level of integrity you hold onto now and the sense of responsibility. I get it. I really do. It's admirable. But you can't fully live when you and Molly are so tightly wound up in a cocoon of secrecy. It's okay for you to open up and let other people in."

"It wouldn't be fair."

He was stuck in his thinking and I knew that neither my tears nor angry words nor any sort of expressive spiritual insights that had filled me during the service were going to help right now. He looked exhausted. I realized it must have taken a lot out of him to share with me the way he did.

I knew nothing more could be said. At least not right now. I got out of the car. Before I closed the door, he said one more time, "Trust me, Anna. It wouldn't be fair."

Leaning over to catch his gaze I said, "I know. And that's the thing about grace. And love, too. They're not fair at all."

I hurried to get inside Rose Cottage but found it difficult to put on a cheery face for my relatives in that small room. Andrew, Katharine, Ian, and Miranda all looked at me expectantly. I'd promised Peter that I'd keep what he told me confidential. It was better for me to say nothing than to slip and say too much.

"Could you help me with one thing in here?" Miranda took me by the arm and led me into their bedroom where she shut the door. "Are you okay?"

"I will be."

"Do you want to talk?"

"Maybe later."

"Okay. Whenever you want to talk, you know I'll be here for you."

"I know." I gave her a hug and pulled away quickly. "Would you mind if I stayed in here for just a little while?"

"Of course. Would you like me to say anything to the others? Jet lag, maybe?"

"Sure. Blame it on the jet lag again."

When Miranda exited, I lay down and pulled the folded quilt at the end of the bed over my legs. I didn't cry. Instead I reviewed all the pieces of the conversation rerunning in my head. Peter had told me about his wild teen years, his summer fling, and how his first year of university had been interrupted with the news that his summer girlfriend had just given birth prematurely. She couldn't care for Molly because she'd been admitted to a drug rehabilitation center.

Peter had looked uncomfortable as he'd told me how his parents had stepped in. They had been the ones who made the sudden move to Carlton Heath and arrived with Molly, saying that she was their own child. They proudly told everyone that they had a son who was finishing university. He was going to become a successful architect. He carried all the hopes and dreams for the family.

My mind tried to imagine what living this false scenario had done to each of them. Peter's parents had worn themselves down to the nub caring for their granddaughter.

Peter had straightened up, studied hard, and gave up his hooligan ways. In his words, God had renovated him. The only hint left of the rogue he used to be could be seen in the way he took center stage in social gatherings. He didn't have to be stoned or drunk to be funny.

The way he saw it, he had made so many people cry. Being in a crowd was his chance to make people laugh.

My heart felt an awful pang when Peter told me in the car that Molly's birth mother had overdosed five years ago.

"So you see," he had said, "Molly is my responsibility completely. She always will be. I can't pretend otherwise."

A tap sounded on the bedroom door. Katharine entered quietly, bringing motherly warmth into the room with her. She sat on the edge of the bed and smoothed her hand over my hair that covered my shoulder.

Neither of us spoke. With Katharine, it seems, words are only her secondary means of communication. Certainly Andrew, in true MacGregor fashion, had made his opinions known to Katharine about what an ideal match Peter and I were. I felt I needed to offer someone in the family some sort of explanation as to why Peter hadn't come inside with me.

"It ended poorly," I whispered.

"Che-che-che." Her calming sound, like the cooing of a nesting bird, settled on me.

"He's determined that he doesn't need me," I went on. "But he does. More than he knows. All he has to do is ask. That's all. Just ask. It's not fair. But not for the reasons he thinks it's not fair."

I stopped before I leaked too many details. It felt natural, however, to pour out my thoughts to Katharine. She listened quietly and breathed over me like a gentle breeze.

I pulled myself up to a sitting position and gathered my hair with both hands, twisting it up into a knot on the top of my head. "I hope I didn't delay the Christmas Eve party for everyone else. Have you started opening presents yet?"

"No. Not yet."

"Well, let's get started, then." I tried to sound chipper.

Katharine reached over and rubbed my cheek with the soft backside of her fingers. She didn't say anything. She didn't need to. Her presence was comfort enough.

Linking arms, she and I joined my other relatives in the living room. I gladly accepted a glass of my uncle's hot Christmas cider. Ian and Miranda began passing gifts around. I hoped the small presents I'd brought for each of them from Minnesota would be up to par with the way they gave gifts. It was socks and bow ties for both Ian and Andrew and lotion and candles for Katharine and Miranda.

Miranda handed me a box with a silver bow. I undid the wrapping and lifted out the handsome leather case of watercolors she'd seen me admiring at Harrods.

"Miranda! I almost bought this."

"I know. I could tell you liked it."

"I love it. Thank you so much."

Andrew took a look at the variety of paint colors all lined up inside in prim little rows. "You should be able to paint not only Whitcombe Manor but all of Carlton Heath with this assortment."

I felt my throat tightening. I wasn't sure what was going to happen now that Peter had made it clear that it was not possible for him to be friends with me. His friends were my relatives. How could I return to this small village in the spring or at any time and not be the source of division?

"Who is ready for some more of my famous Christmas cider?" Andrew asked. He kept the spirits bright for the rest of our Christmas Eve at Rose Cottage. When he and Katharine drove me back to Whitcombe Manor, I was grateful that he didn't try to offer advice or ask any questions. Instead, he talked about how his visit had gone at the hospital with Ian. The two of them had some ideas on how to expand their appearance next year by adding the Rochester Carolers to the agenda.

I kissed them both good-bye and was able to make my way to my upstairs bedroom undetected. I closed the door quietly and pulled the drapes wide open. It made the room much colder but I didn't mind. I wanted to look out and see the faint dots of twinkling stars above the treetops. I wanted the stars to look down on me the way they'd looked down the night of Ian and Miranda's wedding when Peter kissed me.

I pulled the comforter off the bed and wrapped myself up in its warmth. Positioning my cocooned self by the window, I gazed down on the shadowy garden. I wanted Peter to be standing there, ready to toss a pebble at the window or hold out his hand, inviting me to dance.

But he wasn't there. All that remained were shadows of what had been.

If Peter's firm declaration tonight was going to end the fairy-tale dreams I'd held on to for us, then on this night of all nights, I wanted to look out at the stars, close my eyes, and dream one last dream. I told my timid heart to go ahead and remember what it felt like when Peter had slipped my hand into his pocket and the thrill of hope flowed unhindered between us.

I stood alone by the window, just one more person in this weary world, quietly rejoicing and longing to once again hear the angels' voices.

I didn't wish upon a star as I stood there, gazing into the night sky. I didn't dream a fairy-tale dream. I did something real. I prayed. I prayed for Peter because in my heart I had only one true Christmas wish on this O Holy Night. I wanted Peter's soul to feel its worth.

Chapter Twenty-Four

A steady, muffled thumping sound roused me from my deep sleep.

"Yes? Who is it?" I squinted in the brightness of the morning light that was flooding into the room.

"It's me."

The sweet and squeaky voice could only belong to one person.

"Come in, little mouse!"

Julia scampered across the wood floor in her nightgown and bare feet. "It's Christmas morning!"

"Yes, it is." I pulled myself up into a sitting position.

Julia had a Christmas stocking in her hand and a delighted smile on her face. "What did you get in your stocking?"

"I don't know. I haven't checked yet."

Julia went to the post at the foot of my bed where a stocking was waiting for me as well. I'd noticed it the night before when I went to bed but didn't check it for goodies. Julia handed me my stocking and I patted the comforter, indicating that she should come sit with me.

She climbed up on the tall bed and poured out the contents of her stocking and then my stocking's loot a few inches away. With her arm she marked a crease in the comforter between the two piles as if to ensure that we wouldn't get our goodies mixed up.

"You got a Lion Bar, too! Look! We both got one. Lion Bars are my favorite. We can eat them now. Do you want to eat yours now?"

"Before breakfast?"

"Of course, silly. It's Christmas! We always eat what's in our stockings before breakfast. Markie already ate his. I saved mine so I could eat it with you." She bit into the prized candy bar and looked prim as a princess, sitting cross-legged on the end of my bed. Her hair had gone fuzzy and her closed lips turned up in a grin as she chewed merrily.

I followed her lead and bit into my crumbly candy bar. I looked around the lovely guest room and reminded my bruised little heart that this was the day I was letting go. I'd do so privately and quietly. Prudence would be proud of my decorum.

About an hour later, after I'd taken a little extra time getting ready for the day, I joined the Whitcombes in the drawing room around the Christmas tree.

Ellie had tea and toast for us and said we'd have a small feast before noon so why spoil it with a heavy breakfast?

"When Margaret lived here," Ellie told me in a low voice, "I never would have gotten away with breaking the tradition of a formal Christmas dinner. She was keen on everyone sitting around the table. I am, too. It's just easier for me to serve quiche with sausages and pastries instead of making a ham with all the trimmings along with the Christmas pudding."

"But we still have Christmas crackers," Julia chimed in. She'd been tuned into what Ellie was saying even though she was across the room with a wrapped gift in her lap, patiently waiting for a full audience before opening it.

I remembered Julia explaining to me what Christmas crackers were when Julia pointed them out at Harrods and Ellie said they already had ones for this year at home. They were small paper tubes that were gift wrapped with twists at the ends. Julia had described to me the way they snapped when each end was pulled at the dinner table and a small gift would float out.

I was glad they had kept that tradition. I was curious to see how it played out. The predominant Christmas tradition with my parents was the Swedish bread, the *yule kaka*. I tried to calculate the time and wondered what my parents were doing right then.

What will my mother say when I return home and tell her I can't return here in the spring? What will Ellie say when I tell her?

I brushed aside the discomforting thoughts and sat in an open chair beside the Christmas tree and waited for Julia to open her gift from me. The winter sunlight was making an effort to come through the clouds and filter in through the window behind the tree. Every time it broke through I could feel a bit of warmth.

Julia recognized the purple notebook immediately and squealed when she looked inside to see the drawings of Princess Julia.

"You can color the pictures any color you want," I said. "Except the pink macaroons on page three. You must color those pink."

Julia came over and threw her arms around me with an appreciative hug. "Thank you, Anna. I really love this. Look, Daddy. It's a book about Princess Julia. That's me!"

I sipped my cup of tea and gazed out the window. I wondered if it would work for me to take a lot of photos of the manor before I left. If I took enough, from enough different angles, I might be able to do some nice drawings for Ellie. I wouldn't have to return in the spring but I could still keep my word and deliver the much-anticipated sketches.

"We've all opened our gifts from you," Ellie said. "So kind of you. I love the apron. It's perfect."

"Here, Anna." Julia handed me a beautifully wrapped gift. "This one is for you."

"Thank you." I put aside the thoughts about taking lots of photos. I knew I could talk it all through with Ellie later. My alternative plan shouldn't be announced on Christmas Day.

The gift was a beautiful blue-and-white scarf. Julia announced that she helped her mother pick it out for me. For someone who dressed in her own quirky, eclectic way, Ellie certainly had accurate taste when it came to selecting gifts for others. I put the scarf around my neck and watched Mark open a gift from his parents. I noticed the wrapped-up book I'd created for Molly was still under the tree, right where I'd put it the day before.

I decided to nonchalantly remove the book and not leave it under the tree. It seemed best to take it home with me. I could always mail it to her for her birthday or simply leave it in the box under my bed along with the other two copies. Miranda was the only one who knew about it. If I asked, I felt confident that she wouldn't say anything.

With the wrapped book in my hand, I made an excuse about needing to go upstairs for something. As soon as I stepped into the entry hall, the chimes sounded for the front door.

"Anna?" Ellie called from the drawing room. "Are you still there? Would you mind answering the door for us?"

"Sure," I called back. I pulled open the heavy wooden door and saw Peter standing under the arched entry in the alcove.

"Happy Christmas," he and his family said. When Peter saw that it was me, he quickly lowered his gaze.

I was at a loss for words because after last night, I didn't think Peter would show up this morning. And if he didn't come, I had wondered if his family would still come.

But they were here, with a tray of appetizers and several gift bags in hand with lots of white tissue paper sticking out the top.

Peter's parents stood behind him, waiting to be invited to come in. Molly stood next to Peter, holding his hand. She was wearing brand-new, shiny Christmas shoes and they were red!

"I hope we didn't come too early," Peter's mom said.

"No, your timing is just right. Please. Come in. Edward and Ellie are in by the Christmas tree with the children." I nodded my hello to Peter's mother and father.

Molly entered, looking up at me as if she was trying to figure out who I was and what I was doing at the Whitcombes' home.

I leaned over and smiled at her. "Hello, Molly. I'm Anna. I like your shoes very much."

"I have red shoes." She held up a foot to show me.

"Yes, you do. They are beautiful red Christmas shoes."

Molly saw the gift I was still holding and must have recognized her name that was written in large letters on the gift tag.

She looked up at me and excitedly asked, "Is that present for me?"

I hesitated for a moment. I could feel Peter looking at me. Molly's eyes were fixed on the present.

"Yes." I handed it to her. "Yes, this is for you. Merry Christmas."

She threw her arms around my neck and hugged me. "Thank you."

"You are very welcome." I bit my lower lip. I didn't know if I'd done the right thing by giving it to her. But it was the red shoes that got to me. I knew she would be elated when she opened the book and saw that Molly the little lamb also had red shoes.

I let my gaze slide over to Peter, who was taking the book from Molly and adding it to the other gifts in his hands. "We'll open this later, all right, Molly?"

"I want to open it now."

"I know." He patiently and firmly held on to the gift. "After we sit by the Christmas tree with the others, we'll all open our gifts, okay?"

Molly released her grip on the book when she saw Julia coming into the entry hall with the purple coloring book. "Molly, look what I got. We can color it together. It's a Julia the Princess coloring book that Anna made for me."

"I have red shoes." Molly held out her foot to show Julia.

"Those are beautiful," Julia said appreciatively. "I've never seen such beautiful red shoes in all my life."

Molly grinned. "They are red."

"I see." Julia took Molly by the hand. "Do you want to color with me? All my special colored pencils are up in my room. Come on. Let's go."

The two girls made a cute but humorous team, trying to charge up the stairs while holding hands. Molly wanted to stop on each stair and look down to admire her shoes.

Peter had slid past me. He took the tray of appetizers from his mother and headed for the kitchen. He still hadn't made eye contact with me. I took that to mean that this was the way it was going to be. Today we would have to move about in the same circles, share in the same conversations, dine at the same table but he and I would not be friends. I felt the same anger return that had sizzled in me in the car last night.

Even complete strangers look at each other in an encounter like this. I didn't expect you to kiss me, but come on, Peter. If you're going to show up here, you can at least look at me.

The door chimes sounded again. This time it was the MacGregor clan waiting on the doorstep. Katharine had a large basket of food slung over her arm and Andrew carried in a stack of wrapped gifts. Miranda had an equal amount of gifts and food. Ian toted the largest open box of all. It appeared to be brimming with more food.

"We didn't want to run the risk of any of us succumbing to malnutrition on this happy day," Ian said.

I laughed. As flustered as I'd felt around Peter, I now felt back at home with "my people" as Miranda had called them. It was going to be a happy Christmas no matter what. I was determined to do my part to make it so.

Chapter Twenty-Five

O nce the formidable MacGregor clan was inside, they made themselves at home, dropping off food in the kitchen and gifts in the drawing room before gathering by the fire with the rest of the guests. I followed Miranda into the drawing room and stood back as she slid several wrapped gifts under the tree.

Peter's parents were seated on the love seat, in a formal, nice posture. Ian and his parents had taken the sofa and Edward and Ellie were seated near the fire. Peter was standing by the hearth, the way Ian had when he'd made the announcement about their upcoming secret blessing.

"I wonder if I might say something." Peter cleared his throat.

Miranda and I were standing beside the tree. I glanced around the room, trying to gauge everyone's expression to get a hint as to what was going on.

Peter looked over at me for the first time that day and made eye contact. I felt a fluttering sensation in my heart.

"I want to say something important to all of you. I had a long conversation with my parents last night." Peter nodded to his parents as if giving them a final chance to stop him.

Neither of them said anything. I thought his mother looked as if she might cry.

"The thing is, the time has come for me to make some changes in my life. They're overdue. Long overdue. I didn't sleep much last night. I have been wrestling with a number of issues."

Peter nodded at his mother again. "As a wise woman told me, 'A heart at peace gives life to the body.' My heart has not been at peace for some time."

Miranda inched closer to me and gave my arm a squeeze.

"I've come to the conclusion that in order for me to have that peace, I need to tell all of you the truth. The thing is, you see, is . . . well, it's Molly."

I held my breath.

"You have all known Molly as my sister. The truth is, in fact, that she's my daughter." He paused as if waiting for the room to draw in a collective gasp.

No one flinched. Katharine exuded her naturally placid expression as if she'd figured that out long ago. Andrew let his lower lip jut out slightly and then gave a nod. A few pieces seemed to fall into place for him upon receipt of that information.

None of the Whitcombes seemed startled in the least. They'd been a family that had weathered enough shock of family secrets when Miranda showed up. They had nothing but grace and understanding for anyone who was trying to set things right. Grace and peace did reside under this roof.

Peter's mother was crying. His father looked concerned.

Peter rolled his shoulders back and kept going. "You see, when Molly was born, we thought it best to deal with things the way we did for a number of reasons. I'd be glad to share those reasons with any of you if you're curious about the details. My point in bringing all this to light now is that I decided last night that I need to live my life openly, without this secret being the weight that continually pulls me down. Molly doesn't pull me down, understand. It's the cover-up that has weighed on me all these years. It's robbed me of my peace."

Peter looked to me with a clear-eyed expression of relief. I smiled at him. He seemed to have the look of the actor who played Scrooge. When Scrooge awoke to the sounding of the bells on Christmas morning, he was radiant and energized with freedom and great hope for the future.

Peter must have faced the Spirit of Christmas Yet to Come with his parents last night and when he woke this morning, he was a changed man.

Your soul felt its worth, didn't it? You don't have to stay in that cocoon of secrecy anymore, Peter.

His expression seemed to cloud over slightly. "It's been quite difficult for my parents, as you might imagine, for many reasons."

I immediately thought of what Miranda had told me about how Edward's mother, Margaret, had chosen to move in with her daughter rather than stay in Carlton Heath with Miranda once Sir James's secret had been revealed. I hoped Peter's family would stay right where they were.

"That is part of the reason why I wanted to share this with

all of you today. You are our closest friends. I'm hoping you will have the right words of comfort for them."

Katharine was the first to lean in and offer her calming words.

Peter stepped over to me and said, "May I speak with you in the hallway?" He nearly tripped over a wrapped gift under the tree. When he looked down, he saw that it was the gift I'd handed to Molly at the door.

Peter reached down and picked it up and for some reason carried it with him to the entryway.

He motioned that we could sit on the stairs. We sat next to each other on the second stair, neither of us speaking for a moment.

In just the last three minutes my mind had been filling up with hope-infused wishes the way a great balloon fills with air before it's ready to be released into the heavens. If everything had been made right for Peter during the night, he must have reevaluated his conclusions about us.

I wanted to hear what he had to say but he was locked in on the gift.

"When did you get this for Molly?"

"I didn't get it for her, exactly."

"What do you mean? Isn't this from you?"

"Yes, but, well, you'll see when you open it."

"Do you want me to open it?"

"It's up to you. If you want, I can rewrap it so that Molly can have the fun of unwrapping it."

Peter didn't hesitate. He pulled back the paper and held the book and stared at the cover. For a moment he didn't move. He turned to me slowly with tears in his eyes. "Did you do this?"

I nodded.

"When? When did you do this?"

I told him the whole story behind the book as he turned the pages and absorbed each image. He had just turned to the last page when Julia and Molly came scurrying down the stairs.

"Molly, come here," Peter said. "Have a look at this book that Anna has made for you."

Julia stopped on the fifth stair and took Molly's hand. "Did you hear that? Anna made a coloring book for you, too?"

"This one has the pictures already colored," Peter said. "Come, Molly. I want to show you your new book."

I got up so that Molly could situate herself next to Peter. Julia sat a step higher and looked over Peter's shoulders.

"She has red shoes!" Molly excitedly pointed to the lamb on the cover.

My folded hands rose as I watched the tender scene unfolding on the grand staircase. I pressed my thumbs against my lips and I tried to keep my delight from leaking out. Julia and Molly sat perfectly still, quietly captivated as Peter read the storybook to them.

Miranda had left the drawing room. She slipped over closer and stood beside me. "They love it," she whispered. "Look at Molly's face."

Peter got to the last page and Molly said, "Read it again."

He looked up at me with glistening eyes and gave me a smile that expressed all the thanks I needed.

Miranda squeezed my elbow and whispered, "Ellie thinks it would be good if we could put out all the food in the dining room now. It's a little tense in the drawing room."

"I'll come and help." As soon as we were in the kitchen, Miranda stopped me and said, "Well?"

"Well, what?"

"What did he say to you?"

"He asked when I wrote the book and I told him. Then he read it to the children. He likes it. I know he likes it."

"No, I mean what did he say about you coming back in the spring? You hinted at something last night at Rose Cottage. I got the feeling that the tense conversation you had with Peter was about your coming back."

"He told me about Molly last night. He said it wouldn't be fair to invite someone like me into his life."

"What did you tell him?"

"I told him that grace isn't fair. Neither is love."

Miranda wrapped her arms around me and gave me a warm, sisterly hug. "I want you to move here, Anna. I want you to live here always."

"Me, too," I whispered, fully aware of what it would mean if such a wish came true.

Miranda pulled back and looked at me. She was beaming. "I'm not the only one who feels that way..." She patted her middle and then stopped as the kitchen door swung open.

Chapter Twenty-Six

$\mathcal{E}$llie whooshed into the kitchen. As soon as she saw the two of us, she came close and said with a wide-eyed expression, "Was that not a big surprise! I think Peter is going to see lots of good come from his decision to let the truth be known. Lots of good. Especially for Molly. They said they told her this morning. They're not sure she understood but it was important to Peter that he told her. It's the best Christmas gift I can think of for anyone."

Miranda quickly added, "I agree. Every little girl should know who her daddy is."

Ellie's hand went to her mouth. "That's right! Oh, my. We do have a tradition of going for the big reveals around here on Christmas Day, don't we?"

When Ellie said "big reveals," Miranda subtly tapped me with her elbow. I tried to curtail my grin, knowing that when we all sat down to eat the small feast in the dining room, Ellie would be over the moon about the next announcement.

Julia bounced into the kitchen. "Mummy, we need the Christmas crackers. They aren't on the table in the dining room."

"Oh! Right. Where did I leave those?" Ellie clapped her hands together. "They are in a box beside the desk in the study. I left them there the day we were doing the program for the play. Julia, will you go get them and put one around at each place?"

Julia was about to go about her glad task when she stopped and put her arms around my middle. She gave me a hug and said, "I love my Princess Julia coloring book. But if you ever want to make a real book about me some day, I should like it to be about a pony named Julia with long, long hair and big blue eyes like yours."

"I'll keep that in mind."

Ellie had already gone into high gear getting everything else we needed pulled together and carried into the dining room. I couldn't stop smiling as I helped get the serving dishes delivered to the dining room where the table was set beautifully with Christmas china. Julia was skipping around the table giving every plate at least one Christmas cracker. Most of them got two.

My thoughts were filling up with all kinds of ideas for more books to write, more scenes to sketch, more ways to expand my artistic endeavors. It made me so happy to think about bringing joy to others by doing something that I loved. I wanted to start dreaming about Peter again but as I'd already told Miranda, he hadn't said anything to me. As far as I knew, he could feel like he'd been set free from the secret he and his parents had been hiding, but that didn't necessarily mean he had changed his mind about me.

Prudence told me to be patient and wait.

And as my Christmas gift to her, I calmly told her that I would. I would wait as long as it took, because a prince like Peter didn't come riding up on a wagon-style bicycle every day.

The group made their way to the dining room and found their place around the table. I was seated next to Ian. Molly sat across from me. Peter was beside her and Miranda was on his other side.

Edward stood and offered a beautiful prayer that rolled off his tongue with the same sort of vibrato that I imagined had been in his father's voice. It sounded as if a great orator was pronouncing a blessing upon each soul that gathered at that table on Christmas Day. He ended with a rich, "Amen."

Mark tried out an attempt to follow in his grandfather's theatrical footsteps and loudly announced, "God bless us, everyone."

All the guests around the table spontaneously echoed, "God bless us, everyone."

I noticed Peter had to assist Molly with getting the food onto her plate. He occasionally glanced across the table to see if I was put off by the process that had to be part of her every meal. None of it bothered me. If Peter understood the extent to which I cared for my Opa all these years, he would know that very little affected me when it came to such things.

Peter seemed to relax after a few moments. He tossed out a joke that made everyone laugh. As I watched, it seemed the metamorphosis was happening. The man he'd tried so hard to hide was merging with the man he truly was. Grace and peace were making friends within him. It was beautiful to see.

I tried to tell myself that no matter what happened next with

Peter, this transformation was worth all the precarious moments he and I had experienced this past week. The Father of Christmas had presented Peter with a rare and valuable gift today. I took joy in knowing that.

Miranda motioned to me from across the table, asking if I would change places with her. I knew she wanted to be sitting next to Ian when they made their big announcement about the baby, so I switched with her as inconspicuously as possible.

Being next to Peter made my heart flutter again. I tried to hold my emotions in check. The next few moments were going to be about Miranda and Ian. All attention should be on them.

Ian tapped the side of his goblet with his knife. The clinking sound got everyone's attention. "Happy Christmas, one and all. I would like to propose a toast."

Julia interrupted. "Please don't start with the adult talking and all the toasting yet. We haven't done our Christmas crackers."

"Yes," Ellie agreed. "By all means. We must maintain a few traditions. Christmas crackers first, then the toasts."

"Crackers and toast," I whispered to Peter. "I thought we already had our meal."

He gave me a funny look, not understanding my pathetic joke.

"Crackers? Toast? Get it? All we need is a little more cheese." I grinned broadly and realized I was doing this because I was nervous. I was telling myself that all was well no matter what. But that wasn't true.

I'd experienced a metamorphosis this week as well. The fairy-tale girl in me had looked into the face of Christmas Yet to Be and knew that no matter how difficult it would be to enter a relationship that automatically came with a little lamb in red shoes, there was nothing else in the world I wanted more this Christmas.

My cheesy grin was still fixed on my face as I stared at Peter, lost in thoughts of my Christmas wish. He seemed to finally get my pun and said, "How about if we leave the dinner show entertainment in the hands of those who know how to work the crowd."

At that moment, it looked like Peter was going to have a little competition "working the crowd," because Mark had pulled the two ends of his Christmas cracker, creating a loud snap followed by the scent of a match being lit. Out of the cardboard tube came a folded-up paper crown and a whistle. Mark promptly placed the crown on his head and began a series of short tweets with his whistle.

Everyone was popping their Christmas cracker, so I pulled mine and found that I also had a paper crown and a matching whistle. I held up the whistle to show Mark and then gave mine a swift tweet.

"You must put the crown on your head," Julia said. "Like this. Look at us! We're princesses."

The pandemonium around the table lasted only a few moments with snaps and pops and silly paper crowns going on and staying on everyone around the table. It surprised me how playful this reserved group had become. I wondered how Miranda and Ian would be able to make their announcement with any amount of seriousness.

"Did you mean what you said last night?" Peter's voice was in my ear and I could feel the warmth of his breath moving down my neck.

"I said a lot of things last night."

"You said that Molly didn't need to be the only woman in my life that I cared about. You said it wasn't fair for me to not even ask you if you wanted in."

I nodded and caught my breath. Turning and whispering back in his ear, I said, "Nothing about your life frightens me, Peter. All you have to do is ask."

Molly pounded the table. She had torn her crown. Uncle Andrew gladly handed over one of his.

"You haven't done yours yet," Julia said to Peter. "You need a crown, too."

He pulled both ends with a crack and out came an oddly shaped paper.

"It's a beard," Julia cried. "Put it on. You got the Father Christmas beard! Hooray! Look, Molly! He's Father Christmas."

Peter complied and Molly, more than anyone else, thought his paper beard was hilarious. He turned in his chair to face me and moved his jaw up and down so that the paper beard was expressing its full silliness.

"Princess Anna," he said calmly, sincerely. "I'm asking."

I playfully adjusted my paper crown, not catching his full meaning at first. Then his carefully chosen words began to settle on me.

He repeated them. "I'm asking if you'd be willing to come back and see if we can find a way to make sure that Molly isn't the only most important woman in my life."

Our faces were only inches away.

"Yes," I whispered. "I'm willing."

He leaned closer and this time I knew he was going to kiss me. Not give me an expression of hello, good-bye. This was going to be a real kiss.

I didn't turn my head. But I did close my eyes.

Peter kissed me, paper beard and all.

"Anna! What are you doing?" Julia's squeaky voice brought me back to the moment and caught everyone else's attention.

Molly started laughing. "She's kissing Father Christmas!"

The room had gone quite still. I felt as if my face must be as red as a holly berry.

Peter reached for my hand under the table and held it tightly as if he intended to never let go.

Ian seized the moment to redirect everyone's attention.

"On that happy note, I would like to offer a toast." He pushed back his chair and stood up, raising his glass. He looked and sounded an awful lot like his father in that moment. "I would like to offer a toast to my darlin' woman, Princess Miranda."

Everyone raised their glass and smiled. Ian put up his other hand. "No. Wait. I'm not finished yet." He glanced at his dad and then back at his wife. His eyes were glistening. "To Miranda and to our wee babe that she now carries within her."

It took a whisper of a second before Ian's words were fully comprehended.

The Scottish Highlands roar that bellowed from Uncle Andrew's chest was enough to have everyone on their feet, rushing to congratulate Ian and Miranda. The joy in that room brought tears to everyone's eyes. Uncle Andrew couldn't stop laughing and spouting something about the rise of "Clan MacGregor." It was a glorious moment.

Miranda was radiant and I was so happy for her.

Peter squeezed my hand under the table. I squeezed his hand back.

"Thank you," Peter said, leaning close.

"For what?"

"You're the only person who ever asked me if I was willing to show myself grace."

"How does it feel?"

He bobbed his head as if the sense of newfound peace and hope was agreeable to him. I could see a grin breaking through the paper beard. "I'd say it feels almost as good as this."

Peter leaned in. He dramatically pulled off the Father Christmas beard and kissed me again with all the tenderness of a man who had just realized that there is nothing fair about grace or about love. As soon as your soul feels its worth, all you can do is receive grace and love as a gift. A very good gift.

This time when I opened my eyes, I knew without a doubt where I would be spending my Christmases yet to be.

I would be right here, at this table, with these people, feeling like a fairy princess in my silly paper crown and kissing Father Christmas.

Reading Group Guide

1. What fairy tales were mentioned in *Kissing Father Christmas*? In what ways did each one connect to Anna's outlook on life?

2. In what ways did Anna's mother encourage Anna's love of art? In what ways did she discourage Anna from pursuing that love? How did your parents encourage or discourage your interests as a child?

3. If you were to visit London at Christmastime, what would be on your wish list of things to do and see? What sites that Anna experienced did you enjoy most?

4. Are you drawn to people like Ellie who seem to have the energy of three women bundled into one with a quirky personality to go with all that enthusiasm? Why or why not?

5. What happened in the relationship between Anna and Peter when they danced at the wedding? In what ways did dancing

together make it easier for them to have a relationship? In what ways did it make it more difficult?

6. Can you remember a time when you had to step out of your comfort zone and perhaps outside of the approval of your parents or friends to begin something new in your life? What happened as a result of your decision?

7. What Christmas traditions does your family or your community keep each Christmas? Which ones do you look forward to each year?

8. What motivated Peter to believe it wouldn't be right to impose his life with Molly onto Anna? What assumptions was he making in coming to that conclusion?

9. What was the biggest change in Anna by the end of the book? In Peter? What does that suggest to you about responding to what life brings to each of us?

10. What can Peter and Anna's relationship teach the reader about communicating with someone you care about?

About the Author

Robin Jones Gunn

The much loved author of the popular Christy Miller series for teens, Sisterchicks® novels, Father Christmas trilogy, and non-fiction favorites such as *Victim of Grace* and *Spoken For*, Robin's 90 books have sold nearly 5 million copies worldwide. She is also a frequent speaker at local and international events. Robin and her husband live in Hawaii where she continues to write her little heart out. She invites you to visit her website at www.robingunn.com.

Robin Jones Gunn's heartwarming holiday novels are now available in a 2-in-1 edition.

FINDING FATHER CHRISTMAS

Miranda Carson's search for her father leads her to England where she's welcomed into his family as a stranger to them. She quickly grows to love them, but will revealing the truth threaten the bonds they've built? Certainly, this Christmas will change the future for both Miranda and the family forever.

ENGAGING FATHER CHRISTMAS

Miranda Carson is certain she's found the home she's always wanted in the village of Carlton Heath—her boyfriend, Ian, is even hinting about an engagement ring. But when her presence leads to unexpected conflicts, Miranda questions whether she really belongs in this cheery corner of the world.

Available from FaithWords in print and ebook formats wherever books are sold.

.